The Whole Wide World

Childhood Tales

The Whole Wide World
World

Childhood Tales

Robert Lalonde

Translated by
Neil B. Bishop

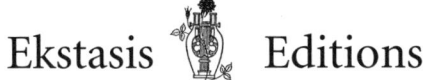

Ekstasis Editions

National Library of Canada Cataloguing in Publication Data

Lalonde, Robert.
 [Vaste monde. English]
 The whole wide world. tales of childhood

Translation of: Le vaste monde.
ISBN 1-896860-84-2

I. Bishop, Neil B. W. II. Title.
PS8573.A3835V3713 2001   C843'.54   C2001-910406-5
PQ3919.2.L19V3713 2001

© Robert Lalonde and Edition du Seuil, 1986, 1998
Translation © Neil Bishop, 1998
Cover Art and Design: Miles Lowry

The original French, *Le vaste monde* was published in Paris France by
Editions du Seuil, 27, rue Jacob, Paris Vle, in 1986.

Published in 2001 by:
Ekstasis Editions Canada Ltd.

Box 8474, Main Postal Outlet
Victoria, B.C. v8w 3s1

Box 571
Banff, Alberta tol 0co

The translation of *The Whole WideWorld* has been done with the assistance of the
Canada Council for the Arts Translation Program. *The Whole Wide World* has
been published with the assistance of a grant from the Canada Council for the
Arts and the Cultural Services Branch of BritishColumbia.

Contents

The Devil Knows	9
Hawk-Eye	23
TheTrickster-Teacher	31
Magic Words	41
Rowboat inthe Grass	50
The "Lip-Ripper"	58
Carnival	73
My Nose Stuck Everywhere	89
Your Mother Has a Visitor	102
The End of the World	114

Almost always, within a family, its dreamer will carry the day.
　　　Gabrielle Roy, *La Route d'Altamont*

If we got to Heaven, we would help forge the thunder.
　　　Büchner, *Woyzeck*

Lord's service by memorizing the two *Ave Maria*, Schubert's and Gounod's, so as to play them in the convent chapel, during May, the month of Mary. We loaded the piano and brought it back. On its own, it played disconcerting arpeggios on the bumpy road. Dad was smiling blissfully, in seventh heaven, tapping on the steering wheel with the mad hand of an orchestra conductor, as though beating the tempo of the ghastly chords the jerking instrument gave off now and then. As we were driving along the marsh and I was busy watching the inverted glide of a heron reflected in the big, liquid mirror surrounded by jackpines, I heard Dad declare behind me, "Anyway, Anne won't need to read any sheet music, she has the gift!"

And indeed, Anne played by ear. Mozart and Beethoven, Father Gadbois, sonatas, lieders, blues, jazz, rigaudons, concertos; and lengthy melodies she made up herself, which carried Mother off into so perfect a dream-world that it often made her drop the salt shaker into the soup.

Until I was twelve, I bore like a scapulary around my neck a little woolen bag, prickly as a burdock flower, containing seven slivers of mica. That talisman was supposed to protect me from the terrible childhood diseases that were feared my fate due to the dark, wine-coloured birth mark on my left shoulder blade and which Edmond baptised "the flying saucer" because, depending on whether I shrugged, stretched out or crossed my arms, the spot would migrate. No matter how hot the weather, I never took off my undershirt, afraid that the red target on my back would tempt some poacher crouching in the grass behind the barn. The origins of my "wine spot" were endlessly discussed. Maybe Mother had often scratched her shoulder blade while pregnant with me, tortured by a fulsome desire for chocolate; or else the headboard, when I was born, was not "pointed north enough"; or yet again, Mother had eaten too much salt, or too many raspberries, or maybe she had walked backwards from the stable the day before her delivery. Incredibly, the hypothesis of the forceps used to pull me from her tormented belly was never seriously considered. For us, myth preceded and transcended reality. Myth preceded all knowledge, and was a pre-scientific philosophy which never lied. Long did I examine the spot on my back, using the two bathroom mirrors: I could see the healed scar of the wing wrenched off me, just before my incarnation. I was sure I should have been born as a bird, not as an angel, as Alice claimed, who tickled my saucer and called me her "cherubim" when her tenderness waxed theatrical. I contorted, washed, and lovingly caressed the sign of my amputation, nostalgic, flustered, resigned. Because of Mother's supposed mistake, her "sin of gluttony through desire" I never, even for Halloween, had the right to candies and sweets. Black and red licorice, lollipops, barley sugar, maple candy, sponge candy, fennel-flavoured sucking candy, klundykes, toffee, Christmas canes, caramel candies and bubble gum, forbidden all those years, made me salivate, slaver, rage, made me sicker and crazier than if I had voluptuously licked, sucked and swallowed them with the serene fatalism of one who knows his frightful feast will be his demise.

To gain the grace of being hauled into the other world, if one happened to die unexpectedly — for anything could happen: cyclones, floods, a fall on a patch of ice, bad hiccups, lightning, choking, getting squashed by a truck — we used to recite, every day:

Saint Mary Magdelene of Quarantine
Three virgins and three ladies go out to the fields
Where have you been, John, my son?
I've just returned from the Garden of Olives.
John, did you see my son, Jesus?
Yes, I saw him, his feet hanging,
His hands nailed
His head crowned with thorns
And his side pierced.

It was never explained to us how this strange prayer that we were to recite, drawing out the syllables as in some languorous lament, was supposed to make the angel at the Pearly Gates wax merciful.

And when sometimes Mother surprised me daydreaming, staring at a knot in a plank in the wall, sunk into a reverie that made me deaf to her calls, she would lose patience, raise her arms skywards, bang them down on her thighs and grumble, "Be careful, Vallier, the Devil hides in the details!"

The Devil hid so well that, as one might expect, I never met him personally. But I swiftly learned to spot the disguises he so often wore to try to approach our place. For example, I knew that, somewhere in the clouds over the farm, if it was snowing and sunny at the same time, he was beating his wife. He might be that black cat glimpsed at twilight on the chicken yard fence, never mewing, even when the dog barked enough to dislocate its jaws just below him. Mother used to say that all cats had "three Devil's hairs in their tail," so we never used to let those baleful beasts, capable of casting spells on us, approach the house. I saw our Mother pale with fright when, one August evening, on returning from the village, our truck ran over a black cat. She would not leave the house for a whole week, certain that the squished feline's soul, hiding in a ditch, would treacherously make her trip, or simply make her mysteriously unable to place one foot in front of the other on the way to church. When we walked past Hector Grandmaison's forge, we could see sparks, red glows, and if we listened too long to the blows the devil was striking on the resonant iron anvil, he might leave his den and grab us by the neck. I always walked past the blacksmith's reluctantly. Nonetheless, one day on my way home from school, I saw him come out. He was in shirtsleeves, a cap perched on top of his head, a pipe between his teeth, and wore a friendly smile. When I took off running as fast as I could, I heard him laugh long and hard behind me: it sounded like the terrifying whinny of a big stallion being tortured by wasps.

The devil could grow and shrink at will. He could just as well take up half the sky by becoming a big black cloud armed with horns and a long forked tail, as hang down till he touched the barn roof, or hide in a bottle of whisky, curl up like a worm in the slightly tart flesh of green apples and then make you sick to your stomach all night. He could enter the house without being seen, steal a tool, a pair of glasses, and even money from wallets and pants pockets. Lurking in the hay, his clawed hands could seize a young heifer by her hocks and, in a flash, "the devil's got into the cows." He could also change colour, turn from red to green, depending on whether he was near or far, make himself whiter than snow to trap a horse's hoof or a truck wheel, appear black behind the window curtains, right in the middle of the night; or again show his big, dark, ragged silhouette on the basement wall above your proper shadow. Usually, he was all alone, but could also come as a foursome; and sometimes all the devils gathered together at the same time to make the tractor break down, make the bales of hay roll into the creek, whistle, send the dust or snow flying, and moan against the windows and in the chimneys. If someone endlessly pestered you, you could tell him to go to the Devil, whence he would never return; or, if he finally reappeared, he would stand in front of you, sad-faced, gaze grim, dumbfounded like a cat who's just seen itself in the mirror.

As soon as something was not going smoothly, it was because the Devil was interfering. We got angry, cursed, and would eventually resign ourselves and say, "The Devil knows what's going on!" Discouraged, we abandoned the dismantled motor on the work bench, fed the pigs with the cake that had failed to rise, sold the cow that kept refusing to give milk — "the Devil knows why" — to the first comer.

And if it was in *us* that something inexplicably went wrong, we had a "Devil of a fever," were "sick as the Devil," had caught "I don't know what, the Devil!"

Strangely, the Devil could be good. For instance, Aldège Charlebois, who came to help bring in the hay, every second summer, and sometimes helped Dad deliver the milk bottles to the village, was a "good devil." He was a tall, shy, frizzy-haired guy who wore overalls clean as a New Year's Day tablecloth, never spoke louder than if he was in the confessional, a non-smoker, non-drinker who rubbed his hands, smiling like baby Jesus, whenever asked to help. Benoît Trottier was also a good devil, always volunteering to put out fires, tame horses, dig wells, take up collection at Mass. He was the one who came, one night, with his big fireman's ladder, to unhook Alice from the eavestrough she was hanging from like a dressing gown on a clothesline. Our big sister was a sleepwalker. She often climbed out her window at night, whistled at by lovers we never saw in the yard, and she used to shout "Fire!" when we caught her before she fell on the iron fence. As for someone who had only one, almost acceptable weakness, such as occasionally smoking a cigar on the veranda or half-heartedly unleashing a curse, quickly gone with the wind, when he flattened his thumb with a hammer, we said he was "not a bad devil."

There were also "poor devils," those who limped, or walked bent over like they had a big bag on their shoulders, due to a handicap or some great, unexplained misfortune. Léopold Girard, the beadle, who never looked at us, but carefully examined the toes of his boots when we greeted him at the church door, was a poor devil. Georges Nolin also, who was called "the drunken donkey." Every Saturday night, his wife went to fetch him from the village inn and brought him back home, raining blows on him with high-heeled shoes. Sitting on the veranda, we watched the drunk — a fat, grumpy, prancing bear followed by its torturing tamer who struck him as she whinnied like a mare, as though she were the one receiving the pointed heel on the back of the bean. Each time, Dad shook his head sadly and muttered, "Poor devil!"

And I could see the Devil, but behind them, on the road. A great, moving, spreadeagled shadow, a black angel, its arm raised and stretched as far as our porch, as though something about our place was signaling him to approach. At such moments, it seemed to me that I no longer heard the crickets fluting, but the bloodsuckers moaning in the grass. The stars were no longer those beautiful fireworks that made Dad exult, but mean meteors that had just exploded in the sky and were going to fall on us and burn us alive.

And then, one day, at high noon, mounted on a tall horse blacker than night, wearing high, muddy boots, his hat askew, the "Devil in Person" came to our place! He reined in his mount at the foot of the stairs, spat heavily in the sand, and lowered upon me two magnificent, dreadful eyes that pierced me through like sharp knives. Just as I was gathering myself for a leap I was not sure I could accomplish, so badly had fear shrivelled my wings, the big man shouted at me, "Ain't your Paw in?"

I shook my head, in a kind of trembling, very approximate "No." The big demon again spat in the sand, got off the huge horse as easily as you scramble down from a knee-high fence post, then came and stuck his two big boots on either side of my skinny substance crouched on the porch step. My heart was beating in my chest like a cat caught in a bag. The big horseman's shadow covered me like a shroud smelling of cigar smoke and curdled milk. I heard him spit again, saw the squirt of dark brown saliva pass by, splashing my arm, and immediately shut my eyes, sure my time had come.

"He's never there when I'm looking for him, the bugger!"

Between the Devil's legs, I saw Dad returning from the potato field, tiny at the far edge of the world, his straw hat floating on the golden stems. He was approaching so slowly that I was sure he would find me dead, squashed under the porch step, when he emerged from the brushwood. I gathered what little saliva still moistened the bit of salted leather I had instead of a tongue and just barely managed to stammer, "There, behind you!"

The ogre turned around so fast one of his boots scraped my chin. He nimbly jumped on his horse, with a sort of hateful grace I admired despite myself and that made all my belly waters churn like when, climbed up in the apple tree, I shamefully watched the bull and cow mating, at the far end of our land. He met up with father in three bounds that raised a cloud of dust which miraculously erased me.

When Dad, pale and withdrawn, joined us at the dinner table as we were finishing, he gazed at me with an eerie look, his pupils swimming like fatty spots on soup, before he declared, in a feeble voice, "That there damn Conrad is the

Devil in Person, Vallier! Never go near him!"

But one did not go near big Conrad Marineau, County Sheriff, the Devil in Person. *He* approached you, as a buzzard does a field mouse in the grass.

Sheriff Marineau was the original source of a strong emotion, half marvel, half terror, that still surprises me today, my legs rubbery and my heart pounding, on seeing certain great Devils so magnificently at ease, roaming about like they owned the whole wide world, shouting their heroic disgust for weakness, doubt, and the uncertain miseries of human love.

The Devil in Person, they say, comes up from behind you, just like the Holy Spirit comes from above. One April afternoon, when winter was retreating and I was walking back and forth through the pine forest like a calf released in a field for the first time, I came out of a clearing to see Sheriff Marineau copulating with his shadow: his pants on his boots, he was growling like a bear while frantically shaking his thingamajig. That wedding of the sheriff and his shadow, a terrible mating of moans and happy shivers in the spring air smelling of horse sweat, encouraged me to undo my trousers and imitate that frightful and easy joy, thirty feet from him, behind a birch tree.

My pleasure over, I scampered, my shorts around my thighs, ashamed of having, momentarily, thought myself to be as great a Devil as the Sheriff. Immediately, he passed right by me, perched on his stallion, his hat askew, a cigar in his mouth, completely absolved of a great sin seen only by fir trees and clouds. No, definitely, that liberty, his, powerful and solid, that frightful ease of a great free Devil, was not for me. The Sheriff burst out laughing and said, his lips rolled up on his innocent ogre's teeth, "Goddam great weather, eh, little guy?"

I nodded and muttered a confused little "Yes," my eyes staring at my insignificant, skinny shadow on the sandy path.

Robert Lalonde

Hawk-Eye

Born a bird at heart, though wingless, I very quickly knew how to soar, glide and fall. And so: to fly. I flew. Which means I imitated my starling brothers whose wings were fully developed and who soared skywards with ease. Sitting astraddle the barn gable, I pleaded with the wind to carry me off, my arms in the air, looking like a sorcerer in a trance. I would close my eyes, and wait. Slowly, fear loosened its grip. Emboldened, I stood up. Already I was reaching the same altitude as the poplar. I was still the same skinny cat just showing off, but soon I would be changed, I was going to cast off my undeserved spell, I was going to fly. My frightening appearance did not yet reveal the swallow I was getting ready to become; but, with the help of the gust of wind I was hoping for, I would be miraculously freed of my weight, and off I would soar. "You can't always expect guarantees in life, you have to allow for chance," Dad used to say. After all, conquering the sky could not be any trickier than making our mare swallow Percheron blood boiled with rusty nails, or counting, three evenings in a row, twenty-one shooting stars in the sky, or enduring seven whole days with a slimy toad tied to my belly with deer sinew, to ward off poison ivy itch.

Already, I could see the dog, way down below, like a cricket in the grass. His barking and whining did not bother me any more than a snake's hiss when I was walking on the ground. Calmly, I reached the edge of the roof, my foot lightly touching the half torn-away piece of sheet metal that mimicked thunder when it banged. I used to close my eyes long enough to recite the prayer to Saint Mary Magdelene of Quarantine, stretch out my arms to catch my coat, and finally dive, deeply swallowing something that smelled like the bottom of a burned pot.

I was flying. I was flying!

For Anne, Edmond or the dog who, now and then, watched my flights into the clouds, I tumbled down, period. And at full speed, the tail of my coat like a kite around my feet, my mouth wide open as if to swallow flies. Edmond would come running up to my crow's carcass crushed in the grass and declare, in a laughing voice that revealed the merciless compassion he felt at any unreasonable enterprise, "No progress, sparrow! I timed you, you lasted four seconds in the air, like yesterday!"

The dog would whimper, leaping and twisting his hindquarters around me as though I were a partridge shot down in the hay. The big blue sky laughed its free birds' laughter, and the wind continued to make my coat fly. I got up slowly, as though I was coming out of a sort of death that had not fully wanted me. My legs still rubbery, I would go out to the field. I was going off to be a "scarecrow," as we used to say about one or the other of those "poor devils" who, gesticulating madly and talking to the woodchucks, occasionally crossed our pasture, haunted by some unfathomable misery — and surrounded by wasps.

I would prance though the field, brushed by butterflies, whipped by tall stems of cat's-tail grass. At such times, I was keenly aware of the ardent uniqueness of my existence. I had flown, and would fly again. What did Edmond, Anne and the dog know of my need to leap into emptiness? Joy, fear, the desire to have done with my own weight: all our emotions are mysterious, to others as to ourselves.

I used to return to the house, raked with scratches, my mop of hair stringy as hay rope. It was supper-time. I was a guest who made the others uncomfortable. I had flown, and tomorrow I would glide. A bitter secret surrounded me. I remained silent, haughty, misunderstood, all alone in the world. The charm, the frailty of my legend formed a halo around me, to everyone I showed the mask of a blissful martyr. My hope was indefatigable. Surrounded by jealousy, I dreamed of my next flight, caressing my "flying saucer" with my fingertips.

In winter, it was easier. The soft snow welcomed me, and I long remained planted in the downy drift which I rode like a cloud. Evening was falling. I stayed there, sunk into the snow shining with a thousand stars I delighted in counting. Above the black houses, the sleeping trees gesticulated like ghosts in the great polar night. Then I would go into orbit, brushing comets, soaring through the shining dust of distant galaxies.

Discouraged by the excessive brevity of my glides, I

began to fall with a parachute. But my machine came apart too quickly and I would land, after a jump scarcely longer than when I stretched out my coat, with my head and shoulders enveloped in an ugly, rusty bat's wing that scratched me bloody. So then I undertook to sew myself a parachute with jute pockets and hay rope. The wind up there immediately turned my sails into a kind of big rag that hurtled me into the grass, bundled up like a leg of beef on a butcher's hook, and suffocating beneath my chute. I tried to jump with a sheet, whose four corners I held firmly in my fists. The pocket swelled like a balloon, and sometimes I drifted as far as the edge of the field, still too quickly, I felt: obviously, I was too heavy, much too heavy. Then I jumped using a sort of hot-air balloon made of chunks of tire tubes sewn together with bootlaces. This gadget was indestructible; and, once, I managed to float long enough to count all the barns along the road. But that was all. So I undertook to hang from the clothesline, or climb to the top of telephone poles. Swallows would swoop down at me, the wind made me cry; but finally I became aware of what, in broad daylight, the birds could perceive. Like a ship's boy on top of his foremast, I could forecast both good and bad weather, sound the alarm when a storm was approaching. I felt extraordinary dizziness in that blue, empty space, all alone at the planet's peak, watching changes in the air, no longer confined to the ground where people moved so pathetically, constantly flattened against things. I twittered on my perch, chatted with the starlings who disdained me, made flute sounds with the warblers, whistled with the breeze that made me move like an ear of grass on the tip of its stem.

I also began to listen to Mass from the church rood-loft where, far below, I could see the ant-like gesticulations of the priest and his assistants. I brought my thumb and index finger to my eyelashes and pinched the priest at the foot of the altar, the assistants, the holier-than-thous in the first pews, whom I reduced to insignificant little people in a tiny theatre of gnomes. At will, I disposed of others' distant movements, I created puppet comedies, I was the puppet-master concocting events for the Lilliputians taking communion, sending them into a frightful dance lit by a candle no larger than a match. By the time the priest chanted *Ite missa est*, I had managed to shrink all the faithful, and to make them play a tale that had little to do with the mystery of Jesus' sacrifice. I continued my fable, progressing along the road, my eye rivetted to my fist curled into a pirate's spyglass and through which I could glimpse the tiny houses, the dwarf cows, the miniature barns and infinitesimal men and women walking, seeming to goose-step hastily off into the void at world's end. I eventually stumbled on a pebble, bumping Dad's hip, and then the world swelled hugely and I was again a gnome in a universe of giants. I immediately shrivelled, awkward, trying to match my gait to my father's gigantic stride as he pulled me by the sleeve and hoisted me into the truck with one arm, as though I were nothing, and a nothing weighing less than a feather. I would half-shut my eyes on the immense fields and too-tall trees; and then I would see the bird, floating in the vast empty lake of the sky. For a moment, I succeeded in staring at the whole county with that bird, from an amazing altitude. I could even see the little elf, perched on a bale of hay in the back of the truck, his face uplifted towards me. But right away the wheels would hit a bump, or a pot-hole, and my poor, dusky vision was restored, limited to a wall of rusty sheet metal, my father's back, or else a big fog of leaves speeding wildly by, whipping my face on their way.

By dint of seeing me constantly perched, or with my eye buried in my fist as if I were using opera glasses, Dad decided that there was something wrong with my eyesight, and took me to the doctor. Seated in a big leather armchair, more comfortable than our living-room sofa, with a big wooden spoon over first one eye, then the other, I made out letters and numbers on a wall. I deciphered all the signs, right to the last tiny ones at the bottom, making no mistakes and never spotting the slightest spider nor zigzagging thread. The doctor congratulated me with a good tap on my shoulder, but Dad immediately dismissed my victory by saying, "That kid there is so sly and sneaky that he learned the letters by heart, while our backs were turned!"

I did not protest: I wanted glasses. I think I was secretly hoping to acquire the serious, concentrated look of a grown-up with my specs on my nose tip. And what if they gave me an even closer-up view of birds, and maybe moon craters, rings around stars?

I awaited the glasses like you hope for a miracle. I remember that the stove hissed a lot, that winter; and each time, as superstition demanded, I rekindled my desire. I was counting on some sort of magic, all the while pretending to move, speak, eat and sleep like an ordinary little demon. I counted the snow crystals landing on a branch of the spruce tree in the schoolyard, convinced that, with glasses, I would count thousands more, clearly discerning the very complicated geometry of those perfect stars. I would also enjoy close-up views of the wool in the clouds, the beginnings of a butterfly in its cocoon, the undulations of a carp on the pond bottom, the eye of a falcon on the hunt, the burst meteors deep in a horse's pupil. I stared at the tortured, dense universe; presaging the end of its mysteries, I was convinced I would finally eliminate the dreamy distances depriving me of an endlessly-dreamt-of harmony with reality.

One spring morning, irises flowering around the mail box post, they finally arrived. I scampered into the field with the package and stretched out on the young grass to see, one last time, the clouds as far-away and fuzzy. My glasses resting on my tummy, I indulged myself in the sadness of my inadequate eyes staring at the mysterious billows hooked to the top of poplars and spruce. With a tightening in my chest, like a sinner about to undergo conversion, I shut my eyes on a fuzzy sky that I would never see again. Then I slowly put on my specs, ceremoniously setting the two flexible, freezing little branches around my ears. I counted up to thirty-one — uneven numbers bring good luck! — and suddenly opened my eyes. The cloud, that big fish-elephant overhead, with its jagged ears, its half-a-tail, was exactly like the big, fabulous beast I had just a moment ago made out for the last time. Horrified, I rolled over onto my stomach, stretched out my new gaze towards the edge of the woods, where the mottled trunks, swaying patches of light, black shadows at the foot of the oak, were strangely similar to the brightly coloured stained glass window I had seen before putting on my glasses. I stood up to examine the field: each stem, each corolla, each fly on each leaf appeared identical to its pre-glasses self.

To think I had expected to finally be able to make out the stars' gestation, the wind's birth in the sky's crimson depths, spot from afar bees swarming and pollen floating, see the dance of infinitesimal spider webs on the barn wall, examine a cricket caught in dew, a snake's teeth closing on an aphid! The world, through eye-glasses, remained fuzzy, distant, inscrutable. The buds on the branch tips continued to sway in the wind, mysterious, unfathomable. The field mouse still ran through the grass, invisible to me. My toes sunk in the mud still ressembled those little white, wizened worms with ants no bigger than grains of sand climbing onto them. I snatched the glasses from my nose and threw them into the brush: I heard them fall on a stone, with the faint noise of fine chinaware falling off a garden table.

I returned to the farm, my eyes half-closed on the foggy universe. I was condemned to climb back up the telephone pole, to hang from the clothesline, to jump off into emptiness in poor imitation of bird flight. I was condemned to live on earth, amid a huge, moving dizzying, maddening mixture of shapes and colours.

Exactly seven summers later, Anne found the rusted glasses. She brought them into the house, atop her basket of raspberries where they looked like the limbs and antennae of a large, disjointed grasshopper.

The Trickster-Teacher

Jérôme Boileau was my best friend. He used to laugh when he walked under ladders, ran with a pair of scissors in his pocket, gluttonously swallowed the black threads snaking across his vest. I was always surprised to see him return alive, when I'd left him after one of his sacrileges. But Jérôme, miraculously, would survive his frightening profanations; and, each morning, awaited me in the orchard. He whistled to call me, and, looking dejected, watched me approaching, incredulous to see his friend come out, unchanged, from that "haunted cabin," as he had nicknamed our house. Eyes big as quarters, Jérôme would touch me, listen to my heart, shake me and eventually declare, "You're not dead?"

"Why should I be dead?"

We used to climb up the apple tree, each find his own branch, and straddle it.

"Yesterday, when I left your place, I moved the clock hands."

"So you were the one!"

"The small hand and the big one on midnight. Your mother always says that when midnight comes before eleven, it means that the youngest person in the house'll croak that night, so I thought I'd see a ghost come, this morning."

"My Dad noticed, and set the hands back."

"Oh, so that's it!"

And he would burst out laughing, tormenting me splendidly. I was supposed to beware him. Mother said that red-heads were all liars, that they were on this earth "to tempt the doubters and confused." Jérôme, true enough, looked every bit the horned angel with his bristling cowlicks, his magician's smile, his shady plans. As for me, I was a doubter and confused, beyond the shadow of a doubt. Jérôme would unerringly spot the glow of uncertainty troubling my gaze and immediately get excited. Terrorized and marvelling at the knowledge I had lit that fire, I would listen to him, ready for any madness.

"I found a nice big pile."

"Where?"

"In the stable, where else!"

"A pile of what?"

"Of shit, natch!"

The plot gradually became clear. The wind tousled my friend's red locks, blowing them onto his pale cheeks. I sniffed at the air with its apple smell, nodded my head, seized by the adventure, scared but happy, already spellbound. We would fill a bag with the pile, at noon, when the men left the stable for lunch. Then we would hide the bag behind the shed, where no one ever went. At dusk, we would recover the bag and take off across the corn field.

"You wait for me there by the field, in the hay. Me, I'll cross the road, climb onto the porch, steal the newspaper and matches, then meet you…"

I felt good, like that, listening to him relate our next nasty trick, scenting the breeze, the stench of fire oozing from my friend, from his pale skin speckled with little moons the colour of fence rust.

That very evening, crouched in the brushwood, we watched our victory: ol' man Thivierge opening his door, jumping with both feet onto his burning newspaper, wallowing knee-deep in cow dung, filthying his best pants, splattering his potted geraniums.

"That'll teach him to look down on us, the old swine."

Because the Boileaus were not only red-heads and liars, they were also, of course, "dirt-poor, mean as weasels, and as dangerous as the Spanish flu." The warnings came too late: I already loved Jérôme. As yet undefineable dreams were beginning in his company. No one would ever rid me of the feeling that Jérôme was to me "as necessary as a hearse to a corpse," as Dad would say. And also, my friend was convinced that I would manage to fly. He used to say, with a sly smile, "Once you get the hang of that trick, you'll show it to me!"

But as for tricks, he was the teacher, and I obeyed.

Hot summer afternoons, we would tie his grand-father to his rocking chair. With a thick hawser, we bound him up like an evil pirate, filled his vest pockets with stones, and ran down the porch steps to go hide in the raspberry bushes, where we watched the old guy's contortions when he awoke tied up like a ham roast. He would swear, shout for help, ricochet off the porch planks in his chair, making as much noise as a bear shut up in a shed, vociferating curses at the two rascals he hated himself for not having drowned like new-born kittens in the gasoline barrel behind the garage. Mother would rush out from her dairy-work, holding up her skirts as she crossed the field to free the grand-father. As she twisted the hawser around the porch post, she would peer into the back of the garden, trying to see us, all the while concocting with the old guy punishment worthy of our demonic insolence. We scampered off from behind the garage, annoying, on our way across the field, the cows staring at us, mooing apathetically. We would go hide in the woods by the river for the rest of the day, as excited and restless as a couple of escaped convicts. Together we planned to run away forever, thought about becoming poachers, highway robbers, Robin Hoods. An enchanted existence as fancy-free outlaws, cleaving the rich in twain and helping famished paupers, awaited us beyond the pine forest where we stopped, breathless, thighs and arms covered with deer fly bites. Heroic life isn't easy. Days were too short. We had barely managed to gather seven or eight logs to build the raft that would take us drifting to the Mississippi or down to Tierra del Fuego, surrounded by mosquitoes, our stomachs shrivelled by hunger and thirst, when dusk slid through the branches like a sinister mist smelling of old mushrooms. Suddenly a star would shimmer in the dark waters of the sky, and an owl hoot high up in the pines. Our hands and knees were scraped, our shoulders crisscrossed with scratches. Suddenly, we could no longer talk, we had said everything, no words remained to sing of our adventure. Dusk seized us like a trap. So, running full out like two Tom Thumbs fleeing an ogre, we went home in the dark of night, our arms outstretched before us like sleepwalkers' to push aside the branches. We were two wrong-doers who, finally, were coming to the end of their triumphs and miseries. We returned to our prisons, where, at least, soup was boiling on the stove and a good bed with clean sheets was waiting.

We endured our penitence, looking like misunderstood apostles, each busy, in his bedroom/cell, planning the next escapade. I would re-read *Treasure Island*, discovering page by page the road I still must travel to possess the dignity of the knight-errant, to whom an archangel or the Devil would send a sign, always, to go yet further. Jérôme would store the treasures brought back from our expeditions on the shelves above his bed: a speckled stone that we thought was gold, an arrowhead which still bore the bison-blood outline of an Apache warrior's emblem, a piece of eagle's nest fallen from a rock, a bottle of whisky dating from the bootlegger era, a knife whose handle was carved into a voluptuous young woman.

One day, my friend's mother, at the end of her mercy, overtaken by unquenchable rage, piled all our trophies up in the yard. (I could not, of course, take home our booty because, as Mother said, "When you pick up something left lying around that doesn't belong to you, your arms shrivel and fall off like dead branches!") After pouring a generous amount of turpentine on our treasures, the old bag flung a lighted candle into the pyre. In an instant, our precious collection rose in grey smoke with a stink of scorched pig. Jérôme stayed angry for a week, shouting shrieks like a bobcat caught by the neck from his barricaded bedroom. When they finally set him free, he ran down the stairs like a madman: neither his father, mother nor even me could follow him into the field where he immediately disappeared, as though carried off by the Devil.

He did not return to the farm until three months later, with a big beard, broadened shoulders; and stinking of cheap whisky. Confronted with the unexpected, fearsome man reappearing on their veranda, neither Mr. nor Mrs. Boileau dared utter the slightest hint of reproach or welcome. The new, bold lumberjack appearance of my friend was just as imposing to his former disciple, who had hoped he would return looking less of a barbarian.

Then began other lessons in which I learned that I too must free the evil six-gun I had been hiding since forever, unbeknownst to me, if I did not want my noble ambitions to be permanently extinguished. Jérôme showed me how to gulp down moonshine as easily as pump water, to fight a beastly adversary whose role he took, rushing at me as ferociously as a mad bull, and to recite by the light of the fire he now lit each evening, exactly on the spot where our trophies had blazed, hymns we invented in which the word "torture" rhymed with "departure," "school" with "cruel" and "pretty girl" with "missile." I couldn't get over it. Not only was I too becoming a man, but an ardent savage who, from now on, would face up to his parents, priest, and school teacher, my eyes bright with a fearsome glow like the pupils of a wolf on the prowl. I learned to smoke three cigars in a row without gagging, to swear like a construction foreman, to whistle at our female neighbours as I walked along the road with big, swaggering steps, my boots unlaced and a cigar in my teeth.

Supplies brought back by Jérôme-the-Wanderer from his escapade in the city included, among other treasures, two or three pictures of half-naked women in a window or on a bar stool. Together we planned their conquest, and fled with them to the ends of the earth. One morning, we got off a freighter full of bananas or oranges, each with a broad on his arm, to lead a great life on some laid-back island where no one would ever require we account for anything.

Of course, Jérôme took off first, and alone. The night before, he had certainly shown me, with a frightfully unmistakable gaze, a newspaper page showing a clumsily drawn Union Jack and the proud figure of the Unknown Soldier, head held high, rifle on his shoulder. Stumbling through a speech full of big patriotic, incendiary words — the call, defence of the homeland, conscription, duty, victory — Jérôme had explained to me, as in a dream, destiny challenging him, armies crossing the Old Country, battles in dust, sex behind barns, cannon fire, bayoneting flesh-and-blood enemies with souls possessed by the Devil, glory, medals, blistered heels, whisky swilled down with comrades-in-arms, in the light of shell-fire. I thought he was drunker than usual, and that he was just rambling. You don't go off to war at twelve, and especially not to the ends of the earth. The next day, his mother, pale as a ghost, handed me a good-bye letter that my soldier friend had left me like a holy relic. In it were the same barbarous words, astonishing clichés glorifying the fate that had precociously seized him, like some rare disease. He promised to write to me about his epic with the full details of his brave adventures as jungle sheriff, from the land he was going to save from the Devil's claws and which bore the name of some exotic spice: South Korea.

Evenings, that autumn, I lit our fire in the field, smoked the three boxes of cigars that were left, and continued to dream, alone, of our happy, unceremonious arrival on our paradise island. Wild cats prowled about me as though I were a woodchuck suffering its last twitches in the grass, doomed to die before dawn. My harmonica wailed in my stead, so to speak, and I saw the irrevocable end of my youth in the dying coals that the feeble breeze refused to resuscitate.

I knew he was lost, long before receiving that first and last letter from that famous Korea which was, in fact, a sawmill in some faraway village where Jérôme was cutting and piling logs, surrounded by luckless travellers stopped, like him, in their heroic advance by very ordinary misery. The saw had eaten one of his arms and, simultaneously, all his mad dreams of glory. No longer, of course, did he write of the beauty of bomb fire nor of pretty girls taken between sand bags, but of the horrid whine of the saw, the wood chips red with his blood, the black sky outside his hospital room window. The Tearful Epistle ended thus:

It's today, Vallier, that you should show me you flyed. But I'm ascared it's too late. I got just one wing and it ain't beatin' too good.

I scarcely knew what to do with my anger. I spent the lengthy closings of my winter days in the woods, pretending to shoot at the hares slothfully fleeing my ghostly approach through the spruce. Then, a little before Christmas, a very clean and not very talkative worker came to our place to tell us, in his awkward, solemn jargon, that my friend had vanished into some hospital for the handicapped, somewhere in town. I smashed the idiot's face long before he finished his sinister errand; which led me to spend three days in the county prison where big Conrad Marineau kept filling my cup with his own moonshine that sent me into limbo, where the illusions we have been foolish enough to let escape twist like worms in our fingers.

What is a friend, if not that angel some unknown God adds to your shadow; and then you cast upon the earth a huge, fabulous, invincible figure? You have become stronger than one of The Magnificent Seven, your hopes are inexhaustible. You look, smell the air, listen and touch with an attention increased by the living presence of the other, you become the powerful beam of a big searchlight. Together, you never lose, you wander with passion. You do not run about the fields, you stroll along the Path to Paradise. Your every word, and his, comes at just the right moment, followed by radiant silences. Come from the heart, the voice seeks the heart, finds it. You are like two trees in the wind who never complain, their leaves mingled, hair through which runs the cordial hand of hope.

Only our old words remained to console me. Everything turned against me. I suddenly came to know that feeling of absolute disgust at the thought of continuing, a disgust that filled my chest with putrid water. I was twelve, I was sixty, I was all alone in the world. A long night of doubt and dread, when truth seemed false to me and the false true. Beneath so empty a sky, my tearful carcass was a pity to see. People came to sit on my bed, uttering those phrases one speaks to the dying, phrases sprinkled with wise warnings and despondent encouragement, like so many knife thrusts finishing you off.

I never saw Jérôme again, except once in a while, in a train, or the depths of a tavern, where certain red-headed guys showed me the sea-blue eyes and half-smile of my lost friend.

And then, I don't know how, I ran, caught a branch, then another, and escaped from my trap. We help each other up, love one another, someone, and then someone else. Marvels endlessly stretch before us, farther, higher, marvels that we sense without seeing them. And other angels still further off, beyond a bend in the road, are waiting for us to put ourselves in their hands.

Robert Lalonde

Magic Words

She was walking all alone on the beach, beneath a large teal umbrella. Not only was it not raining but the sky was devoid of the slightest cloud, the sun burned so brightly it hurt the eyes. Later, much later, I would learn with considerable astonishment that, on that day, Miss Saint-Aubin was walking beneath a Parasol. A shadow just for her, a shadow-her, her shadow. The pretty word "parasol" will always, for me, conjure up Miss Saint-Aubin, that long shadow walking quietly on the sand under a rain of light she sheltered herself from as from a downpour.

To go to Sunday Mass, Dad and I — who both were "more than a little shaggy" — had to stoop to prevent our heads from striking the laundry store sign which overhung the sidewalk and bore red-lettered, English words under a fairy-tale prince's crown, "Crown Laundry." I must have been about fifteen the day I learned that the poor unfortunate victims of skull fractures had not necessarily hit their head on the sign in question.

If some one surprised me, calm in my corner, watching

or listening to the visitors chatting and gesticulating in the living room, or else crouching in the grass watching for my cousin crossing through the corn to come find me, I used to mutter, "I was doing my blank nothing."

For me, you did "your blank nothing" when you were trying, usually unsuccessfully, not to be noticed. "I'm doing my blank nothing, you're doing your blank nothing, he's doing his blank nothing." And I could see that blank nothing very well, very clearly. That false transparency, that colourless nothing — me or someone else — awkwardly concealed in a door-frame, or behind a curtain of grass, lying in wait.

I was taught by my aunt Yvonne that, when you changed clothes in the middle of the day, on returning from Mass or before visitors arrived, you "unchanged," and that the old junk you burned in the barrel behind the shed was "carbage." My aunt Yvonne treated a Mexican "captus," covered with deadly needles, like the apple of her eye; and would put her underwear to dry on the "storve" in her living room full of all sorts of china dogs and cats to "horld" the doors. She taught me that one must pay the milkman and the shoemaker "cash on the nose," and never get into a discussion with an elected politician or the parish priest without "watering down one's vine." And I could clearly see the coin stuck to the milkman's nose, the hallway vine being watered when the priest came to collect his tithe. Just as I heard — without his screaming revealing its mysterious meaning, however — the auctioneer shout "three bucks, going once, going twice, going three times!" While Mrs. Lacasse or Miss Thibault shouted with relief, before approaching the little stand where the guy would ceremoniously enrich her with an old wash board, or maybe an extraordinary lampstand jig-sawn to look like a water hyacinth. Once, twice, thrice lucky, perhaps, the lucky chosen one, the radiant woman so congratulated on returning to sit among us, her face three times more transformed than by the Host of Holy Communion. I used to cry out, "Good things come in threes!" to show that I too was involved in the miracle of the three-buck lamp or the enigmatic wash board, both three times worthy of being thrown in the "carbage." People would look at me dumb-founded, thus convincing me that I would still have to endure many a slight before the little Pentecostal flame would descend upon my head, the flame that enables you to understand and speak all the languages in the universe, all at the same time.

Twice a year, I heard news of an uncle I did not know. The envelope was so thick and long that it stuck out of the mail box, and often I needed a knife to remove the bird droppings hiding George VI's six wan faces. These missives came from so far away that they reached me after the blizzard or the lunar eclipse my Uncle Hubert wrote to me about had left us, or else long before they arrived.

My uncle, Mother's brother, was an Oblate of Mary-the-Immaculate, on a mission along the banks of the Giant River — "Nakotsia-Kotchô," he specified in his lovely, slender handwriting — "in the land of the Hare-Skin." I did not know why I was the one to whom Uncle Hubert addressed his humble, valiant missionary's epistles, full of the

The Whole Wide World

Northern Lights, enraged bears, drunk Indians, saintly, extenuated but hardy Brothers, their cassocks torn by thorns and dog fangs, of spruce-covered islands, fish egg cakes and sleigh trips that lasted months, from Good Hope to Notre-Dame-de-Bonne-Espérance and as far as the desolate steppes of the North Pole.

I did not know this Uncle Hubert "hide nor hair," as Mother put it when I decided to ask her why the missionary wrote to *me*. She crossed her hands on her chest, raised her eyes, as though the answer to my question was hanging from the living room ceiling light, and eventually murmured, "I don't know, but I'm sure it's not bad luck. Hubert was so kind!"

"Was," as though the Oblate had long ago succumbed to the cold at the top of some glacier and was writing me from Heaven.

Equally dumbfounded, but more down-to-earth, Dad would say, "Nail the letters above the door-frame and read them often. You never know, you might end up knowing how to write like somebody educated."

So the letters were a mystery, and would long remain so. They had something to do with the din of a destiny which, however, I felt was not to be my fate. I read and re-read them until I knew everything about the great miseries and little joys of the "pioneer far from his native land." I even eventually caught, like a sickness, the Oblate's rich, flowery style which brought me very good composition marks in school, and which still shows through, they say, whenever I relate the slightest incident, which I manage to tell in endless detail, like an odyssey.

The first of these long letters from the Far North began thus:

My dear Nephew,
God, it would seem, after creating the beautiful lands of the Whites, noticed that between His hands there was still a lump of poor-quality soil. Not knowing what to do with it, He threw it far away, saying scornfully, "That's good enough for the natives!" That is where I'm writing you from today, from the Arctic Circle where wary moose, nomad caribou and great whitefish reign.

For a month now, it's been an endless winter night. The sun, which disappeared from the horizon November 30, briefly reappeared at noon, January 15, as a wan glow, and our Lord alone knows when we may glimpse it again. Deep in this eternal night, the land of the Hare-Skin is a vast cemetery where men, animals and things, wrapped in snow and silence, emerge from the shadows like ghosts.

Uncle Hubert's letters convinced me that there existed other worlds than the one I scampered about in every day, my eyes staring at marvels I couldn't see. Words had perhaps not, after all, been given to us just so we could hide our thoughts and emotions.

I used to emerge transfigured from these letters, even more knowledgeable and dazzled than Edmond when he straightened up from his workbench, after his experiments, his face blackened and his eyebrows scorched.

My pupils, like a still-damp calf's, with which I still

The Whole Wide World

gaze today upon reality's uncertainties, came to me, maybe, from my frenzied reading of Uncle Hubert's philosophical, geographical, geological, theological, northern letters. The good priest's eloquence was such, that I myself came to want to be a missionary-explorer-world wanderer: I too would go encounter that famous Arctic light that burns your eyes and rids dreamers of their every superstition.

My dear Nephew,

Way up on the sixty-fifth parallel, the air is so pure that it makes you drunk like a quart of that Mass wine that my brother and I used to glug down when we were children, on the rectory steps (as you must have done: all young boys want to escape their minds so as to enter their dreams, truer than life...).

I am aware, from far away, of your outlandish, excessive behaviour, and of the painful weight of your desires. You are right. The universe — your village, its surroundings — is not a painted backdrop your boat will penetrate some fine morning when you decide to go see the ends of the earth. There will be a whole other side of the world, seas, islands, people who dry out their dead in urns, animals with fur softer than your own skin, flies that can put you to sleep forever with a quick dart; and all sorts of songs more harmonious than music itself and sadder than All Souls' Day in a church in ruins, struck up by men and women wearing blood-spotted furs and who carry on loving conversations with the moon and stars, all day long... What you cannot yet see, I know you can guess, already you suspect the other side of things... Time does not exist: only haste and immobility, desire and dread, daring and renunciation...

Tomorrow, my brethren and I will harness the dogs and plunge into the dense tundra fog where we shall sometimes be able to make out the blurred halo of the still-living, still-warming sun, even when invisible... Dear child! Hope, and you will leave... Oh, if you could see a flock of Arctic terns soaring like a white cloud over the crimson ice!... Love your solitude and your beautiful, haunting dream of the far away: that shall be your salvation...

I went around reciting them aloud, to the dog, the cat, the trees and the fences, those mysterious evangelical letters, convinced that their words were infinitely more than words, that they were, in fact, so many calls, the growls of lions and tigers reaching me from the ends of the earth, the echo of some threnody chanted deep in the heart of a volcanic crater by demi-gods swathed in light. And I would answer with reedy whistles, laments that tortured my throat, dumbfounded stammering, fearsome twittering approved by mad swallows and thunder rumbling above the pines.

I was drunk with words, and have remained so. I have never been able to sober up. Those poisonous things are all-powerful; their ambrosia caused my once-and-for-ever, *ad vitam aeternam* madness.

And then, one November morning, when a big armful of letters was strewn on my bedroom floor (I read and re-read them, both before falling asleep so as to guarantee that I would have an explorer's dreams, and on awakening so as to begin my day remembering that finishing the great map of the world awaited only my coming) I surprised our sister Alice, sitting at the kitchen table, bent over a book with its cover torn off and yellowed pages, from which she was copying a passage onto a sheet of stationery that I easily recognized. She was using a large feather obviously wrenched from the big gander pecking in our farm yard. On seeing me, Alice quickly slammed the book shut and buried the letter in her apron pocket. Too late. I had already, had finally, understood. That day, shut up in the shed, I read from beginning to end *Letters from the High Arctic,* by the Reverend Father Hubert-Paul de LaDurantaye, Oblate of Mary-the-Immaculate, a missionary to the Baffin Island natives. A downy first snow was falling outside the window of my hideout. I didn't in the slightest notice time going by. They had thought they would fool me, play a trick on me: in fact, they had carved out, for me, a Royal Road through the brushwood.

I reappeared at dusk, in the kitchen where my family awaited me, an untouched plateful in front of each and every one, their eyes widened by the glow of remorse and shame that came too late. I sat down, ceremoniously, as though our ordinary supper was really a great banquet held in my honour. I calmly swallowed my dishful of stew, not deigning to look at anyone, prouder than a canon priest invited to share a pauper's meal. No one dared conclude the story, express the moral of the nasty tale. I got the last word, which I kept for myself until dessert. Then, when they no longer held out any hope of hearing me, I rose, gracefully deposited my napkin on the tablecloth, where it landed with the silken whisper of a priest's stole caressing the lace on the Holy Table at a Palm Sunday Mass; and declared, in a deep voice which had never been mine but would be every day henceforth: "All in all, that was a very good idea! Now I possess all the vocabulary I need to make you pay for your incredible stupidity!"

And I went out the door an accomplished writer, excited and well-avenged, my founding book under my arm. The made-up uncle had taught me to spell out my desires, to ward off all those obstacles that constantly prowl around inspired dreamers.

I would go on — alone, since fate so ordained — beyond the sixtieth parallel, the land of the Northern Lights and the dreams you spell out beneath a frozen moon. And I too would turn it all into bushels of books, more believable, more amazing than the Holy Gospel.

Rowboat in the Grass

I experienced my first forbidden spasms in a boat floating on two sawhorses, in the field behind the house. Dad built boats all year long, night and day. Rowboats, barges, canoes and rafts floated permanently in the field, their prows splitting golden shafts in summer, snow banks in winter, their hulls riding the breakers of some great, invisible river wherein swam field mice, hare and shrew. Those craft were for Ti-Ouelle Nolet who, thanks to our father, owned the most impressive fleet in the county, at the service of tourists and fishers from the big city who flooded in every summer. In hot sun, rain, snow when the boat, covered with a tarpaulin, looked like a collapsed teepee woven from spider webs, gaily coloured with pigeon droppings, Dad would saw, glue and nail, singing as he stood in the perched carcass of a boat frame, his arms in the air and talking to himself like Ulysses answering the mermaids. August evenings, beneath the light bulb hung on the lowest branch of the poplar tree, amidst its frightful glows in the grass as it drew his giant shadow on the house, our father looked like an ogre busy feasting in the belly of some huge dead fish.

Cathou and her brother Gérald were two mischievous little devils as supple and saucy as otters. Together, they possessed the secret of those tickles and swoons that deliver your body from its drowsiness as easily as Dad set wild cats free by opening the door of the cage where Edmond shut them up. My brother's experiments and tests on the poor beasts usually wound up with the death of his guinea pigs in their wire cage, forgotten in the back of the shed and which we would discover, their muzzles bloodied, their claws half ripped off and their bellies stuck to their vertebrae from the hunger and thirst they had endured without complaining, sometimes for weeks and weeks.

Cathou had the brown little face of a cunning angel nestled in the black foam of a mop of hair that looked like it was made of the frayed stuffing they used in buggy seats, and which cascaded wildly down her back to where her buttocks began. She fidgeted like algae in water, glided in the air, did not walk but swayed like a branch in a soft little breeze that blew only for her. And above all, she would lie down, gracefully dying in the bottom of the rowboat, her mop of hair covering her like an animal's fur, and would immediately come back to life, awakened by her hands which, all alone and on their own initiative, would first lightly caress her, climbing her thighs, then suddenly frenzied, jerk up her skirt in one motion to bury themselves melancholically in the black, frizzy little lair nestled beneath her tummy round and golden as the "bum of bread" that we ate Sundays, after Mass. The sides of the rowboat hid from the whole world, first Cathou's trout-like quivering, then our little games as a threesome in the bottom of the rowboat. If the neighbouring farmer, high on his tractor, came to ogle at the boat swaying ever so slightly on its sea of blond wheat, he could only catch a glimpse of two little boys playing at fishing, their heads lovingly bent over the boat bottom where a truly extraordinary pike was wriggling.

Gérald's skin was milk-white and his head the colour of the ripe grasses caressing the rowboat. People said that his sister and he were of two different fathers, both long gone, one a Métis and the other maybe "English," both "skirt-chasers, pimps, heartless jerks," of course. Gérald would stare at you with big porcelain eyes the misty blue of pre-dawn, that never blinked even in paroxysms of pleasure or anger, like a doll's eyes. He barely paled as his half-sister caressed him or when our faces touched as they approached Cathou's little breasts (which had suddenly popped out of her sweater) warm, fuzzy as peaches. Our games set off the alarm among the starlings and the warblers, the mosquitoes and the black flies: an anthem of chirping, skimming and buzzing would surround the boat where, wrapped in scents of sawdust and wood glue, we experienced wilder storms than the hurricane that would soon put the rowboat through the wringer in the middle of a lake.

The day my uncle Bérubé took me fishing with him on the river for the first time, it was aboard one of those rowboats Dad made and which had more than once sheltered our threesome's languorous skirmishes in the field. While my uncle was casting his spoon, I stared at every detail on the bottom of the boat where I could still glimpse Cathou's writhing hips and Gérald's cat-like stretching. We must surely have left traces, tracks, little slices, bits of skin, hairs, dark spots on the wood from sperm or sweat, some treacherous sign of our frolics. And I would keep both my hands, like restraining belts, on the hard-as-a-branch little appendage inside my underwear.

"Do you expect the pike to jump into the boat all on its own? Watch the floater, dumb-bell!"

My uncle would laugh, smoke, cast his spoon again, convinced of my perfect innocence. Lost in my marvelling doubts, left scatterbrained by the red-and-white floaters bobbing in the current, I let my incredulous gaze float upon the water, convinced that if I dove in, the river would not wet me. I used to caress the varnished wood of the rowboat with a tenderness and desire known to me alone, my head resonant with my friends' moans, that little beast with two bodies that swept me along with it into a formidable, slow-motion combat, there on the bottom of the rowboat.

Nights, I tossed and turned in my bed, caught up in the memories of our squirmings in the boat. Then I would get up, tip-toe downstairs, push the screen door open as slowly and gently as a ghost, and head off into the tall grass, naked and feverish as a lover about to embrace his love beneath the stars. I would climb into the rowboat like some hurricane survivor, as damp with sweat as though I had really been in the water, and stretch out on the cool wooden bottom that would tame my heat. The sides of the boat carved out a piece of sky for me that I watched as though from the depths of a well into which I might have flung myself in a dream. An oval firmament crackled overhead with will-o'-the-wisps that challenged my energy, tortured my lower belly and filled my hand with wild enthusiasm. I would relieve myself, as happy as when I rolled with my two accomplices on the sun-warmed planks. I visualized acrobatic, amazing gestures and positions. I dared, I ventured into a passion-filled bog where our three bodies, but also other, unknown, arousing anatomies squirmed together in an orgy of caresses and suckings that wrenched groans out of me, like a puppy in mud. My eyes glimpsed fleshy, glowing parts that I could not have imagined. My hands rummaged through shiny furs that I had never before seen on baptized humans. My nostrils filled with odours of peat, daisy hearts, corollas of wild, poisonous flowers I had always been sensible enough, until then, not to sniff. My spasms made the rowboat pitch, the stars flew past, the whole sky became fuzzy, comets burst forth, the moon's halo grew, the entire universe expanded, exploding endlessly: I was at the origin of the formation of a new galaxy, I was going to be sucked up into orbit, drifting forever in that pitch-black, very distant infinity where the satellites roamed.

Mixed in with my fantasies were bodies and faces that I had never seen, except innocently, on a farm, at church or else simply on the road in front of our place. The strong-armed hired hand who lodged above the shed, the blonde braided girl who sat by me at Mass, our neighbour's son who plowed shirtless, surrounded by gulls, perched on his tractor like a gladiator on his chariot. These bewitched folk abandoned their routines to join me in satisfying appetites which, just like me, they did not possess in their calm, everyday activities. I, and I alone, invited these innocents to unbridled lewdness that they would surely never have dreamed of, given their natural moderation. I was a demon; and, just as my aunt Yvonne invited people to her *salon*, I invited people to Hell in the rowboat, sometimes three nights in a row, leading a frightful orgy under the bewitching full moon. I seduced the placid, drove the virtuous into a frenzy, dragged reserved farmers, honourable housewives into a satanic storm in the bottom of the boat, under an extraordinary night sky that tolerated with diabolical ease that party, those mingled, passionate bodies, those panting centaurs and werewolves in heat.

At confession, once a month, I would admit — without going into the details of my frightful talent as master of perversions and without hoping for the slightest leniency from the priest, who listened to me as he stroked his stole with his fingertips — that I had sinned through desire and involved quiet souls in my sensuous visions. The poor priest, aghast, nodded his head and whispered to me: "Be more specific, more specific!" But I went no further, stopped cold by shame and especially by the appalling certainty that I would do it all over again at the next full moon. My confession itself was another sin: as I was confessing my ribald ruttings, my tool grew hard in my underwear, my face flamed and my back oozed an all-too-familiar sweat. The discouraged old man called the Lord's mercy upon me, and that of Mary His Mother; and, after ten "Our Fathers" and thirty-six "Hail Marys" recited under the big cross from which stared down a most gentle, dying man whom the sun turned so blond as to make the blood of his wounds seem pale, I would run out of church, both forgiven and ready to promptly, joyously endure another beautiful, guilty, turbulent night in the rowboat.

And then, one August morning, Dad found me asleep in the boat, stark naked and my belly speckled with an unmistakable frost. Towering over me, feet set firm and wide apart, cap in hand, for a moment he looked like a sad parent at some youngster's wake, following the latter's death due to a most mysterious malady. He said nothing, nor did I. I grabbed my underwear dangling from Dad's arm and put it on amidst a silence scarcely broken by the larks. I jumped into the grass to be met by busy crickets whose shrill chirping informed me that it must be almost noon, and ran through the field, lashed by the already tall hay, to the shaded edge of the woods where I let myself collapse like a beast struck by a bullet. I immediately heard the angelus ringing, sounding my death knell. I lived out the rest of that day in haughty, inscrutable solitude, busy meditating on the mysterious depths of destiny, surrounded by clouds of flies and mosquitoes sent by God to punish my scandalous wrongdoings.

When the red glow of the setting sun appeared between the branches, I was preparing my disappearance, convinced that a monster lurked within me, that it had begun to show itself; and that, from now on, I was neither a son, nor brother, nor even anyone's friend, but a puppet, Beelzebub's plaything: taking advantage of night and the rowboat, he had seized me.

I no longer wanted what I was, not a soul would have wanted me either, I was sure. The very forest sought to rid itself of me, multiplying its screams, its cracklings, like some huge, invisible brazier. I went home in the pitch black night, crossed the kitchen where everyone saw me pass by like a ghost, an escapee from some ogre's lair, and I went to my room where my bed, chest of drawers and books awaited me; and in the middle of all that, an incredibly gentle, innocent moonbeam. I slept like a drunkard who has sunk to the depths of his bottle, and did not dream. Apparently, my chimera had left me.

The next morning, at breakfast, after staring at me as though I were some unkempt wanderer that you let come in and immediately seat at the far end of the table so you won't catch his lice, Mother shook her head, expressing a kind of dismayed "No," smiled sadly; and declared, with a mischievous tone I had never heard from her, "You should say good-bye to your folks when you go fishing. Otherwise, you'll be unlucky."

Dad laughed first, then Edmond and Anne, and finally everyone guffawed.

Then Mom got up to take care of the dishes. Never again was mention made of my misdeed in the rowboat; and I calmly continued my existence as a rake disguised as a normal child.

Of course, I returned to the boat. I still go back there. And take with me, as I sail the grasses beneath a thousand complicit stars, good, marvellously beautiful, tempting people forever unaware of the charming debauchery they become guilty of, with me and by me, despite themselves. After my orgies, I peacefully dry off beneath the great black sky; and ever the same unknown, snickering, hoarse voice murmurs deep within me: "Oh, the poor innocents!"

The "Lip-Ripper"

Back then, sounds were still just noises. The cries of goldfinch or jays, the whisper of snow beneath sled runners, the mare whinnying, the heifers lowing in the stable, a blizzard whistling in the windows, the drum of hooves against drinking troughs, a plough scraping over ice, rain streaming on the barn roof. And, of course, the songs of voices, murmurs behind doors, shouting in the fields, mumbled responses in church, from time to time a farmer's song as he was sitting on the last bale of hay way at the top of the cart. And, of course, my sister Anne's sonatinas on the convent piano. But music did not yet exist. I knew nothing of it: I would listen, training my ear to it as you build up your arms by lifting rocks, as Edmond trained for scientific magic in the deep darkness of the shed. It might happen that a chant would leave my lips, like the braying of a messed-up motor. That would be when I was walking about thirty feet along the road, unaware, carefree, oblivious to my surroundings and myself. On reaching the poplar or the mail box, I had lost the tune and wasn't even thinking about it.

And again I started listening with a passionate intensity I did not recognize. I would hear a mynah bird whistling as though I were flying alongside it, without realizing I would never forget that hoarse, fretful lament. I used to imitate it easily, repeating the chirps so well that I would be surrounded by twelve annoyed birds following me along the road from fence post to spruce top. Then the bobolink would start up, and I would unintentionally repeat its lament. I echoed bullfrogs, frogs, woodchucks, I feigned owls' hoots, borrowed the church bell's ring to awaken Edmond, took inspiration from the dog's yapping to move the cow away from the ditch. No one, at our place, was surprised by the buzzing, ringing, twitters and diverse moans I uttered all day long and at the drop of a hat. It was not yet music, rhythm, nor melody. The harmonica still awaited me on a shelf in the general store in company with stuffed animals, Christmas wreaths made from vine shoots, and golden boxes full of butter candy. Jos Baswell also awaited me, his "lip-ripper." as we called mouth organs, quietly lying on the workbench in his shop. Jos was still just the village shoemaker, and I was still just that little boy who, once in a while, went to see him to have a pair of boots re-soled, or a leather apron re-sewn.

Sometimes, the silence was such that it made me doubt my own existence. Then, sometimes, I would quietly cry, standing against the barn wall, in harmony with the gray sky and the crows cawing. Music would come, soon now, seizing tunes from the frightful emptiness, reviving desire lost, stirring up those great, free waters that endlessly pour forth from the heart and flow off to disappear in places unknown.

The Whole Wide World

On the way back from school, one winter morning, persecuted by a blizzard, my ears burning, my feet frozen and my hands numb in my cardboard-stiff mittens, I entered the shoemaker's shop to warm myself by his stove on which, permanently, bubbled a pot of coffee thicker and blacker than motor oil. Once the gusts of wind had been repelled by the door, which I managed to close by squashing my bum against it, I was immediately charmed by a sweeter tune than the most beautiful bird song ever to enter my ear. I advanced three paces without realizing it, my toes clamped like a rooster's spurs into the bottom of my shoes, and saw the musician squatting in front of the open stove door, his face gently lit like a saint's in church. Jos had not heard me and a gust of snow enter his shop. He was playing, his back turned to me, spellbound by some sort of intoxication that made him sway as though the beautiful music was cradling him. I could see the harmonica as it extended beyond his head, sometimes to the left, sometimes to the right, throwing glowing rays like silverware on a New Year's Day table. I drew closer and discovered, stupefied, his thick lips quivering as they languorously travelled over the holes in the instrument, with a sort of supple, moist, back-and-forth motion, imitating a wantonly lascivious kiss that even my most audacious daydreams had not yet let me glimpse. From time to time, Jos took the harmonica from his mouth, making a lapping sound like a sheep's hoof stuck in the mud, wiped his thick lips with the back of his sleeve and immediately stuck them back onto the square-holed mouth of the instrument, playing a cooing, drawling, yet syncopated refrain, a passionate rhapsody that his feet also played, making the floor resonate like a big drum.

Despite myself, I began to move my head and jerk my numb arms in a sort of "dancing on the spot," clumsy and capricious, which caught the shoemaker's attention. He immediately ceased playing, buried the beloved harmonica in his shirt pocket and stood up, grimacing as though all his bones hurt at the same time. I realized then that Jos Baswell was old. The shoemaker's body was leaning towards winter, while his music still palpitated with the spring of life. I was overcome by inexplicable emotion mingling blissful admiration and sad pity. I too remained silent. We continued to look at one another, as though we had not yet noticed each other in all the times I had entered his shop to warm up, or to give Jos our shoes to mend. Then Jos spoke. I had never heard him utter any words other than ordinary ones required by his work and by the calmest courtesy. He told me of the infancy of the tune he had just played, in a little Carribean island bearing the name we gave to God in Three Persons: *Trinité*, Trinidad. Grabbing an old boot with one hand and his flat-headed hammer with the other, Jos began to nonchalantly spank a leather sole, talking all the while. I finally noticed the grey, frizzy brushwood on his skull, the wrinkled skin on his hands, the bright eyes in the smoky tan on his face.

I knew that his real name was not Jos Baswell. We used that denomination to label any stranger, any exotic wanderer who one day stopped in a village and, mysteriously, stayed there. At my request, Jos informed me that he had been baptized Archange DeTambel, was born on his

Biblically-named island, had very briefly been raised there; and that, after some cataclysm, some family-scattering tornado, he had taken a boat named "Steamer" with his mother, which had borne him over the most turquoise waters in the world as far as New Orleans, where Blacks were persecuted as criminals.

"But you're not really a Negro, are you Jos?"

"Mulatto, but it boils down to the same thing, my little friend!"

And that word "mulatto" evoked for me some impossible animal begot from the monstrous coupling of old Lanthier's black donkey with some poor white woman ill luck had shut in with the donkey, in the dreadful blackness of the stable at the foot of the sand slope. I did not attempt to interrupt Jos to ask him to untangle those images, for I found his tale marvellous and he seemed determined to tell it to me all at a go. You would have thought that he had been waiting forever for that snowy December dusk and me bursting into his shop, so he could unburden his mind of innumerable, fable-like memories which it had amassed despite itself, never losing a one. As he reeled off his story, his speech changed, and I heard emerging into the world, from his mouth, an indecipherable musical dictionary which, he informed me, was Blacks' speech in the Deep South, a mixture of old French, English, Spanish and other, wild tongues, and which bore the name of a cereal we did not farm in our area: Creole. I learned that his mother had been flogged more than once because she did not always fill her basket to the brim with balls of cotton, that snowy, diabolical substance Jos told me had been used to weave my shirt. He too had been beaten — until his guts stuck out of the wound — for the insignificant reason that he had stolen a basket of peaches at a market in the big city.

"We lived from day to day, you know. On Monday, we made do with what had made us happy Sunday, which was next to nothing. We often would spend two days and nights rocking ourselves and lamenting, sitting on the beaten earth in front of our little house. And using our lips and feet as though our poor shoes held the power to take us to the stairway leading up to Redemption…

Jos described to me a world as ancient as the Biblical Babylon, possessing a short name smelling of hot winds, and which Jos uttered like a litany, stretching wide his impressive lips: the South. Apparently devastated by the North's frightful thirst for money (were we to be counted among the torturers, we who lived, if one excepted my Uncle Hubert's Arctic, in the planet's north?), having lost a war that martyred it, leaving a long, desolate land where only dry peanuts and elegant flowers with poisonous scents would grow, the South had seized language and music which were, Jos proclaimed, the arms of the vanquished. People began to talk about the defeat on their dusty verandas, in the darkness of their cabins. They laid bare their passions with ardour, mixing into the Bible tragedies of ancient peoples and the budgies' chirping. "If music be the food of love, play on, give me excess of it!" wrote the great poet. We played on, hoping that the night would bring us a little peace… That's what we thought, what we wanted, "poor fools"…

The shoemaker's crippled speech sang like his harmonica, articulated by those same thick lips that made the instrument utter a tune which could force the lame to get up and dance, but which Jos said could also lead to despair "all those who go off to seek wool and come back more shorn than sheep."

With Honey Williams and Bud Lincoln, two cronies black as soot, the wonderful racket had begun under the tulip tree in front of the little house, with Archange's harmonica, Honey's tomtom — a sheepskin stretched over an oil barrel — and Bud's cracked voice. Then the trio moved to Black Bottom, Hell's Hole and other rum and whisky bars in New Orlean's French Quarter. After making dogs, cats, lizards, mosquitoes and a few rag-clad children dance, the orchestra obliged tourists wearing Bermudas and sunglasses to wriggle, tourists who could bear Blacks only if they beat out wild rhythms and screeched soulful chants, the only things that could un-constipate those Puritans and remove a bit of their ferocious arrogance as the Great Owners of the World.

I was suddenly carried far away from the rigaudons and soporific church threnodies, far away, also, from the county's taciturn dwellers and their poor, insignificant gesticulations. Jos told me that in the South, the churches were always full of worshippers who wriggled and brayed, swaying like reeds in the wind, chanting their misery to God as loud as they could, their arms stretched upwards. I could imagine how shocked our local parishioners would be if, some Sunday, a procession of shouting, drumming Negroes were to enter our church. I could see myself rising from my *prie-dieu* and following them, swaying, navel naked, waving my shirt like a party streamer, while the appalled priest fled to the sacristy, limping like Lucifer expelled from Heaven.

When I asked him how he had wound up in our village, Jos sighed deeply and stared at me as though suddenly noticing that the little questioner crouched before him was not a zombie from the chronicles of his personal legend, but truly a young, foreign gnome who should perhaps not be told of the calamities of an exile whose causes were lost in the mists of time. He slowly shrugged, sighed again and, just prior to putting his mouth organ back between his lips, muttered "*l'amour*, love, *amor*... Life's beautiful cataclysm with its huge store of frightful inventions!"

And then he resumed playing the same tune, at times melancholic, at others wild, his gaze wandering to torrid, desolate, distant lands, his feet tapping the rhythm, perhaps, of some eternal yet departed passion. Outside, the blizzard still blew, and the windows showed supernatural snow that Jos did not see and that I myself scarcely noticed anymore.

For Christmas, that year, I got a harmonica in lovely, golden gift wrap. I immediately blew three shrill notes that scared me as though I had blown into an old pipe. However, the laughter which followed that first screechy arpeggio did not faze me in the least. The next day, I put on my skis and, warmed by a powerful urge that I shouted to the howling wind and the crows watching me progress like a field mouse through the snowstorm, I went to Jos'. When Jos opened the door, and after I managed to unclench my fingers to show him my instrument, adorned with frost like a Christmas decoration I might have wrenched off the tree before leaving home, the shoemaker smiled broadly and declared, "That'll have to do, for starters!"

And do it did, indeed. On the following Saturdays and Sundays, in the shoemaker's shop, I learned to blow and draw on the harmonica. Jos' music obsessed me, that winter, as a horsefly obsesses a steer. I crossed great rivers and fields, went way off to unknown villages whose cabins slept under innumerable, never-seen stars, I woke girls who had fainted off in hammocks beneath tousled palm trees, glimpsed the green sea through the pines, felt the hot wind of the South flowing over my face, beat the rhythm of desires, getting ahead of myself as though some great love theme was seeping into my body, welling up in my saliva, urging me to such amorous ardour that it made my instrument squeal frightfully. Jos charitably warned me that I would never learn how to play properly: music was "a pretty woman who always remains twenty steps ahead of you," the most expert lips in the world could never succeed in making that puny metal bar full of holes the "cardinal tune," the "indispensable song," which would remain "forever inaccessible." But I played, like I used to fly, compulsively. I let out some unnameable substance, I was no longer that crazy little thing conceived to be separate from the universe: I was playing! Jos glued on soles, nailed shoe heels, and I played in the warm sun of his presence, enduring with ineffable joy his hand on my shoulder, his fingers in my hair expressing my progress towards that unreachable perfection. Once in a while, Jos would pull his own harmonica out of his pocket and, with me, start playing some refrain with neither beginning nor end, which rose, fell, became ecstatic, then languid, flew off to trill high in a Louisiana tulip tree, suddenly returned to our fields to growl with the storm, and did not stop until the clock rang, warning us that it was time for me to ski back to the farm. I got home at dusk, my head full of Negro music, and visions of heavens and hells glimpsed in the extraordinary miaowing of my mouth organ.

With my harmonica beneath my pillow, I dreamed of the skies Jos had told me of, as softly violet as the inside of an oyster shell, and of the yellow and blue birds that flew there, cooing enchanting music that recalled the extraordinary brutalities of love, and summoned one to believe in both angels and demons. I witnessed the Trinity Island volcano spitting enormous bursts of fire, could feel the South's rain, warm as blood, on my shoulders and chest; I was caressed by moss hanging from great oaks like the beard of some giant hung up in the branches. I used to swim in the black bayou waters with glistening Negroes whose white smile, in the night of their faces, taught me that I had not yet begun to discover the miraculous kindness of the human heart, nor the infinite sadness of abandonment. In such dreams, I underwent emotions which my ordinary soul had not imagined. I was like one of those southern flowers which open only at night to get dead drunk on their own scents, then shrivel at dawn, little dry balls no longer smelling of anything. I walked all those nights in streets eaten by the sun, edged by tall tulip trees full of cicadae, and in their shade I swallowed fruits big as hearts of Jesus and that made my saliva squirt onto the ruts left by the carts in the middle of a sand road crawling with lizards. The South was the land of excess and misery, and I knew my heart was made for those contrasts that tear you apart and unshackle shouts and music that suffocate you, if you keep them bottled up. I put the instrument to my mouth in order to reply to the birds along the paths, took it out of my pocket to fill the void when my school teacher fell silent, blew it before supper, after supper, on going up to bed, on getting out of bed: standing, sitting, lying down, I fled to the South where languor was the ordinary mood of all mortals, from richest to poorest, from wisest to craziest. I lamented, exulted, crawled on the ground, flew up to pirouette with the skylarks, dove into ditches; with rats I fiercely gnawed a decaying carcass covered with flies, and in a flash flew with a butterfly along the corolla of a burdock flower which I re-baptized "magnolia," for Jos had convinced me of the unequalled beauty and intoxicating balm of that marvel of a flower bearing the name of some languorous girl.

People never saw me anywhere without my harmonica, so I was nicknamed "Lip-Ripper." They constantly asked me to stick the instrument in my mouth or wrench it from my lips, depending on whether my tunes healed their souls or, on the contrary, worsened the itchings of the music-less next to me when I started to play. Some even went so far as to say that it was not me who was blowing into the mouth organ, but an angel who had taken my place. Often, while the melody took flight on its own, I could see heads looking around everywhere to try to flush out that Vallier who, a moment ago, had been right there in front of them and had mysteriously disappeared at the magical whisper of the first notes. It seems that the smile I wore, while playing, was not mine; and that I bowed my head in an angelic way that was absolutely not naturally me. Little mattered to me such nonsense, which I understood because I did not recognize myself as some music-playing cherubim: what mattered was that I filled or emptied hearts, seized those parishioners (men and women who never noticed me, to whom I could not say two words without them shrugging, turning their backs on me and continuing on their way as though I had said nothing at all), and pulled them along with me out of the future and past, into a radiant, definitive, lasting present. I gathered the secretly worried and hopeful, men and women who dreamed without knowing it. I forced them to remember that maybe we had been put on this Earth for other purposes than ploughing and Sunday mass; and that, deep within our bodies and souls, were mysteries more beautiful and less sad than hailstorms on orchards or the massacre of the Holy Innocents.

Of course, when my tunes ceased, people gazed down at me, the magic gone, terribly disenchanted to finally discover me, the usual Vallier muddled in insignificance and weird delusions. But magic spells, as well we know, are meant to last even less long than roses, and I did not take umbrage at the nasty tirades thrown at me: they reflected people's implacable need to take up life where they had left it, rather than real cruelty on the part of all those good people interrupted in hard work that was not progressing.

"Yeah, well, all that's fine and dandy, but I still haven't hung out my laundry!"

"You're making progress, Vallier, my boy. But you play so many notes besides the tune we know that it ain't even recognizable no more."

"Aline, Marie, Huguette, you still haven't done the dishes!"

"Keep it up, Vallier! You'll be playing in church one of these days. But maybe more often at funerals than weddings…"

"HA! HA! HA! Right on, Aldège! That there music is as sad as *Dies irae* sung by that fat Charles Arbic!"

"Auntie, I want a mouth organ too!"

"Well, first tie up your bootlaces right, silly child!"

"Who wants to come help me put in my fence posts?"

"Yeah! 'Cause with your damn music, Vallier, you've made us awful late!"

Late or early, they had listened to me, the ghosts of their dreams had tugged their sleeves, shown them the South, that Paradise which was never far away, whatever they said or did.

With Jos, I did not have to worry about those so-called apparitions of an angel that took my place and played. "Music doesn't belong any more to the person playing than to the one listening. It's a balm or venom, depending on whether your heart is cheerful or you've reached the end of your tether…"

When we played together, it was always the same breakaway as we soared over Jos' South, become mine too, that land of joyful martyrs, red sunsets and invincible hope welling up with the scent of poisonous flowers. Jos declared in vain, constantly, that he had nothing more to teach me, that I now played as well as Honey Williams or Bud Lincoln: in my eyes he remained the unsurpassable master of glissandos that make your blood gallop, of rasping, discouraged arpeggios he played with his eyes closed — to see all the better our desires and fears dancing madly around a big, invisible bonfire.

One morning, Rose-Aimée Ménard, his neighbour, found Jos slumped over his workbench, his head in a pile of soles still smelling of fresh glue, his hammer fallen on his instep. I had played with him the night before, and had not noticed at all, on my old friend's body, the beginning of the dilapidation that would bring him down. He had simply stopped blowing on his mouth organ before the final crescendo in our favourite improvisation which Jos had let me baptize "The Good Weather-Bad Weather Rigaudon." The melody rose and fell, not ending until one of us ran out of breath. Usually I was the first to lose my wind. That day, Jos had stopped playing, because his heart was on the verge of giving up. And I had seen nothing, sensed nothing, heard nothing.

After long letting them beg me, I went up to the choir loft and played our tune, composed for two mouths. It descended upon the faithful gathered around my friend's coffin: incomplete, insufficient, but very mournful nonetheless, it made the villagers shed more tears than their handkerchiefs and shirtsleeves could wipe away.

I went down South, not long ago. I saw with my own eyes the crimson sunsets, the long groves of magnolias, the paths of red sand, the languid posture of Blacks, men and women, slumped and smiling on old, broken-springed sofas on verandas. I heard the banjos, trumpets and "lip-rippers" play our tunes that I barely recognized, for those people's long habit of playing them without putting into them all the joy and suffering they had endured had left the tunes unable to move the heart.

The South is a country nestled in the body's geography, like a necessary muscle that hurts whether you move or are resting, a second heart that beats both too fast and too slowly. And music rips your soul as it does your lips, for it remembers the land lost, and all the Jos, Buds and Honeys of those arid lands where so much has gone with the wind, that finally only the lips remain to sing of endless abandonment — "life's beautiful cataclysm, with its store of frightful inventions."

My lip-ripper is still and always within arm's reach, and Jos blows on it with me, sometimes, when the weather is too lovely or too bad, too hot or too cold for my soul to bear.

Robert Lalonde

Carnival

Every summer, a carnival visited our village. It all began with a procession of trucks filled with the frightening, rusty old iron of the roller-coaster, giant dolls with straw hair and old-fashioned dresses, big tin butterflies hanging from steal beams long as trees sticking out over the sides of the trucks and ripping low branches off the oaks overhanging the road. The whole kit and caboodle tottered and clanged as it descended the hill, the truck tarpaulins floating like the gaudy flags of those distant countries where children and madmen are kings. I used to tear headlong down the pasture, my heart in my mouth, to join the file of little squirts already following the procession, a long, wriggling, chirping line surrounded by the dust billowing up from the truck tires.

The carnival would camp for three short days, two long nights, right in the church square, sprawling its yellow wagons, its red-and-blue tents, its cages with their overweight grizzlies and frightening bearded women, overflowing into the schoolyard. A big bell, rung by a dwarf who rose high in

The Whole Wide World

the sky with the rope, called the gaping onlookers to enter a heaven full of squeaking rides, phenomenal ugliness, prodigious feats of Herculean strength, slot machines and candy floss that got all over your face like a sweet, sticky spider web.

On Sundays, we went straight out of church into the tents — where genuine Paradise could at last be found, swarming and noisy as a dream. Angels and demons jumped out of little red doors painted with moons and yellow stars, and bore down upon us screeching like heifers tortured by horseflies. I was heart-set on missing nothing of the lavish show, and, the first day, wandered by the trailers and cages, like Noah busy counting the marvels worthy of entering his Ark. My memory was that big boat, already crowded, which I filled with wonders that could help me get through neverending winters, long, hopeless evenings, my personal Floods.

One particular Sunday, I walked past the fortune teller's gaudy cabin without stopping, convinced I already knew everything about the frightful severity that governed our lives — its load of omens and feigned warnings had haunted our home for ages. All I had to do was hold my ear to the wall of the trailer to hear the gypsy woman's deep, hoarse voice whisper to Mrs. Taillefer or Mr. Bilodeau that a devastating paralysis of their left arm, a sudden monetary windfall or yet again some terrible grief would soon hobble the course of their already stumbling lives. Immediately I took to my heels, fleeing the accursed den, and hurtled towards outlandish things which had not been placed on this earth to foretell the future, illness, catastrophes; at any rate, the end of our hopes.

By the old lion's cage, my heart would settle down. On smelling salty leather and hearing the animal's husky voice, I pulled myself together. The old King was still there, circling very slowly around the tin antelope skeleton hanging in the middle of his cage, and glaring ferociously at the frightened onlookers almost touching the rusty bars of his prison. As soon as he saw me, the old feline stopped his crazy circling and limply dropped, holding out to me his open mouth with its chipped canines. His big tongue hung out and his emerald, crazed eyes stared at me with the dazed languor of someone possessed by the Devil, and who has just emerged from some terrible, incomprehensible distress. I became his Jungle Child, come from the rocky desert of his birth land to bring news of his home and family, and to tell him about how legendary he had unwittingly become there, in that brush land of which he remembered nothing and which, nonetheless, haunted his whole, indomitable, sad body. I stretched out my hand, watched by the stupefied onlookers in their Sunday best whom I no longer knew, and gently caressed his big paw with its torn sole and claws worn till they bled. In as hushed a voice as at confession, I poured forth my compliments in what I thought was lion talk but was just a flow of syllables without rhyme or reason, hissing, and as deep as I could make them in the depths of my throat vibrating like an organ pipe. I saluted in him the great, exiled King, lauded his qualities as a sovereign, banished yet still all-powerful. The lion closed his eyes and then I knew he was seeing the golden grass and red sun of his native brush lands. He lovingly listened to my praise, forgetting to shoo off the flies with his tail, then languidly reopened his eyelids, and pierced my own gaze with his huge, liquid eyes, more beautiful and helpless than those of the big, scourged Jesus on his cross at the foot of the road leading up the hill.

The old lion went to sleep and snored, open-mouthed, returned to his native Africa, his crown of rust-coloured hair stirred by a breeze that, to me, smelled of sand and, to him, maybe, of frightened gazelles. I gently let go his paw, legitimately overcome with the emotions of a lion-tamer who has successfully performed his job as big cat charmer; and, for ten cents, I entered the tent of the Fattest Lady in the World. You couldn't see her at first, you had to go through curtains, worm your way between two cables that left your hands stinking of horse manure, climb on top of a banana box and wait for the last drape, with the very ample figure of the freak painted on it, to rise. Children clapped their hands, men whistled, women hid their heads in their shawls, and then an extraordinary silence fell. The curtain rose, you could hear a pulley creaking, and, way down below, as though at the bottom of a pit, slumped on a wooden beam that bent under her like a thin plank, her two huge feet in a wash basin like an impressive pile of wet laundry, the pot-bellied woman, clenching a cigar in her teeth, her thick mane of black hair raised onto her head like a big ball of frayed wool, eyed us with the frightening, black gaze of a sow in a slaughterhouse. The smell of fried tallow and honey-scented soap rose from the pit, where the mastodont stared at us without budging, puffing on her cigar like a lumberjack. I didn't think she was alive, convinced that she was not real, and that they had made a model of this exaggeration of a woman out of a huge block of wax, a gigantic piece of soap. But the freak began to move, sway, lifting the ham of one of her arms to show us a big, elephant's breast and then the other, its twin, even more bloated, its purple areola bristling with long, dark hairs like pieces of fishing line.

The whistles, shouts and banging returned, louder than before: it was like the boots of knife-wielding farmers circling round a pig about to have its throat cut. I had gone in there alone: there was not a shoulder, not a bit of shawl in which to bury my eyes which wanted and did not want to watch. "Just you look at her swinging her tits, buddy! You'd swear they were two cows, one on top of the other!"

"You'd damn well have to roll her in buckwheat flour to see her navel, for Christ's sake!"

"That, my friend, is one mean ton of flesh to have to satisfy!"

The village men, whom I had believed endowed with normal appetites, and with a shyness stronger than their savagery, were so wild-eyed as to scare me, and yet free me from the shame I felt: the shame of so often having the premonition that, deep within me, was a wild animal. Always and everywhere were people worse and better than I. I was but one untamed among others, just another one possessing those powerful, chaotic instincts. Excited by the clamour rising from my fellows in barbarity, I again lowered my gaze towards the freak who was wallowing now in her pan like a hippopotamus in muck, and pulling her hair as though it was burning rags she must wrench from her head. Suddenly, sounding like someone possessed by God and the Devil both, she uttered a lament which echoed in the tent's stifling air like a loon's forlorn cry on a mountain lake. Her ponderous, miraculously awkward gestures were a mix of beauty and horror that made you shiver hard. Again turning my eyes away from that excessively troubling sight, I immediately caught the very pale blue gaze and pallid cheeks of a tall girl standing on the edge of the platform and clenching her skirt with both fists, as though the screams of the ogress and the men's shouts around her threatened to tear her skirt off at any moment. I was moved by that pale, upright, slender, motionless and most beautiful statue which seemed to see from very far away what was in front of her, as you remember a dream, standing all alone by an empty road. I slid along the bench, reached her side and looked her over freely. It was Angélique, of course, I should have recognized her right away. The only woman left in the noisy crowd beneath the tent, Angélique was indulging in the dark pleasure of observing how far misery, silently endured all day long, could drive a human, not made to endure it, crazy and lead her to behave more madly than the worst crackpots imaginable. "Do *you* find that funny?"

I had not realized she had noticed me. I suppose my halo of someone scandalized, excited by the torments he was enduring, must be shining about me, bright as the moon high in the sky. "Not especially."

Answered I very quickly, staring at the large back in front of me as if the simple act of raising my eyes to hers threatened to reveal my inner ambiguity of which, moreover, I was sure she was already aware. However, then I looked at her as though summoned by her insistent attention posed upon me like a net on a butterfly in the grass. I used to often be like that, at the mercy of whoever saw me, flushed me out, showed me in some almost imperceptible way that they knew I existed without seeming to, among other, ordinary living beings. She was old and young, reserved and yet obviously possessed of a propensity for fear as well as joy. Deep in her eyes was that glow I had already glimpsed, once, spying on her as she was gathering wild grasses behind the schoolyard, with the gestures and attitude of "the saint chosen to flower the donkey destined to carry Jesus into Jerusalem," as Mom used to say. Angélique had looked at me then as though she could see the excellent destiny which could still be mine, if I would but let her show me the straight and narrow path.

"It's degrading, and, at the same time…"

She did not finish, probably convinced that I too felt how upsetting were the grotesque movements of that hairy she-elephant ponderously writhing in another world, wilder than our own.

When the freak bent over to show her buttocks and make them quiver like a huge bowlful of pancake dough, Angélique seized her shawl in both hands and turned on her heels, heading for the exit. I followed her, sure that I now felt disgust as tormenting as hers. In front of the church, the sun was shining, the trees had not changed, the river was displaying the same whitecaps dancing out in the open water, as on every Sunday when Mass was the only show offered to the village Christians.

Angélique did not look back to see me following in her

footsteps. She was speeding off like some Cinderella who had just heard midnight strike and was hurrying to reach her carriage before it turned back into a pumpkin. Behind us, the carnival was noisy, dogs prowled around the tents, muzzles raised, tails wagging. I did not at all understand why I was running behind Angélique, beside her shadow. I saw her go down to the beach and plunge into the willows. I heard her speaking among the branches, uttering keening moans as though wasps were after her. I entered the water without worrying about my Sunday boots and immediately saw her, standing on a big rock thirty feet from shore, her skirts blowing in the wind, her hands pressing her head. Again she looked like a statue, Madeleine de Verchères praying, while the waves played the part of the hundred Indians bent on taking her virtue. I floundered through the water to the rock, and boldly climbed to sit almost on her feet. She squatted, not in the least surprised to see me, like a little doggy, beneath her fluttering skirts. In a long, graceful movement like a stem of grass bending, she sat down herself, and raised her head to a sky as blue and smooth as a freshly-painted barn roof. With the voice of an angel I had never heard elsewhere than in my dreams, she said, "He is gentle, he is mean. He is easy to understand, and yet I can't figure him out. But the heart he wants to give me is not made for me…"

This was followed by a big sigh imitating the waves, and then a shake of her head, sadder that the farewell you bid beside his open grave to the uncle you will never see again in flesh and blood. Ever innocent and curious, I asked, "Who?"

Angélique lowered her gaze upon me, two eyes so sad they made me turn my head towards the open water, as though I had climbed the rock just to count waves. She added nothing, nor moved. For an endless minute, I stared at the water, trying to understand the reason for my infinite curiosities, for those calls I answered without ever being sure I had heard them. That extraordinary desire to not just mind my own business took me hither and thither, entangled me in the comings and goings of others for whom I was sure I had something to do, without ever really knowing what. "Will you at least be different from the others, you who are already starting to…?"

Different from whom, and starting to what? Her words floated in the air. Angélique was surmising, suspecting, stating hesitantly. Mom used to say that a cat had swallowed half of Angélique's tongue, and I was beginning to understand why it was the swallowed half that annoyed everyone: that was where the truth was hidden, which she was born to tell us but which she kept jealously to herself, taking on the haughty air of "Joséphine-know-it-all" that turned her interlocutors topsy-turvy and finally made them furious. But I had all the time in the world, I had the patience of a spring stem, I was, naturally, born to experience and know everything. I waited, feet in the water, fingers caressing the smooth and rough parts of the rock we were sitting on, gazing far off, straight ahead, as though, not from Angélique's mouth but from the horizon were to surge forth the words which would ensure that the world — now at a complete standstill — would continue on its way. And then, probably because I had remained rather than leaving her just sitting there as some other guy would have, after ten times starting revelations which ended before reaching the essential,

Angélique began her spiel, a copious spiel indeed. She unleashed on me all the words she had clearly never managed to spit out nor swallow back down for good. I listened, dumbfounded by the miracle that gave birth, in a single head no less fragile than anyone else's, to so many complete sentences, as though they had been ready and waiting forever, and which spouted out of her like the confused speech of someone hit by a stone in the back of his head and wagging his tongue without really knowing he's talking:

"You see, it's not that fat lady, with her blubber and idiocy, who disgusts me. Did you see the men's eyes? Their disgust, but their desire too, mixed together like flour and salt in pie dough? That, that makes me... How do you think a woman feels around them, with her skirt brushing the floor, she holding on to her virtue with both hands, like Little Red Riding Hood being leered at by the wolf? To be disembowelled, be nothing but a soulless carcass for them, gee thanks, thanks a lot! Some other time — that'll never come, believe you me! What on earth gets them so worked up, those bulls not tethered to their stakes right? The apple of Eden? It was eaten long ago! And everyone knows we're not angels, despite the Commandments, the sacraments, Christmas, Lent, Easter and the Resurrection! That's no reason to jump on each other like desperate, famished beasts! You, Charles Boisclair, with your eyes big as a calf's and paws like a fat bear's! You sing sweet nothings into girls' ears with your starling's voice, like the whinings of a wild cat hanging in a neck snare; but you unbutton your pants as soon as the poor girl listens to you! And you, Maurice

Guindon, with your hair like Saint John the Baptist's and your arms like the Archangel Michael's when he slew the dragon, you're worse than the other guy! Thigh always thrust forward, bent to make me sit down on it! I shout at him, 'Get your hands off me!' But the big dummy starts to laugh like a mad horse. If I escape, I can hear him behind me in the field, trampling the grass right up to our place. He stops at the foot of the slope, out of breath, smiling from chop to chop, and bows low to me like the priest during the Elevation. Is all that ridiculous behaviour supposed to make me beg my father to buy the beautiful white gown waiting in Mrs. Dugas' store window? Damned farmers and lumberjacks! A girl is not a tree to fell, or a bottle to chug-a-lug!…"

I could see all that: the bull, sporting Charles Boisclair's face and Maurice Guindon's arms, tethered to a stake in the field; the white gown sitting in the window; the tree-woman being chopped down by the lumberjack; Angélique-the-bottle Charles Boisclair was clenching, getting ready to guzzle her down like a thin flask of moonshine. And also Angélique's sad rage. She had spoken looking skywards, her eyes like those of the first Christian woman attacked by lions, the one you could see on the painting at the back of the church and that left me horror-stricken. Straight off, I remembered my lion in his cage, he too enraged and sad, a victim of the cruelty of men more savage than he; and also the fat show lady who would never have the right to the charitable, ordinary destiny of the farm wife in her decent skirt, hiding behind her kitchen curtain, safely sheltered while she watched the scandals and misery of others. And I could hear, like an echo of Angélique's laments, a buzzing deep in my head that was trying to convince me that no one is ever happy, ever content, that the Devil pursues us endlessly and that even the cicada singing in a heat wave is not celebrating sun-joy, but its fear of the hornet nestled on the next leaf. The universe in which we had all haphazardly been put, men, women, children and animals, was a game of snakes-and-ladders with many more snakes than ladders. It was misfortune, more than happiness, that the tokens on the board had in common. We were more to be pitied than blamed; and yet we could not bemoan our lot, for "that arouses the evil eye" which has the power to bury you "up to your eyeballs in deep shit," and then abandon you there as fly fodder.

Yet the weather was so lovely, the sky so blue, the clouds so fluffy, the birds so merry in the open air. Overhead, life was passing by, laughing with generous, calm indifference. Why had we not been born birds, birch leaves, or acorns, with neither hopes nor memory, tossed around joyously by the wild breezes, the infinite open air? So as to show all that to Angélique, I raised my arm, pointed at the treetops, at the little cloud caught in the branches and that looked like a dishevelled cabbage. I wanted her to fly a little, soar up for a second into that space devoid of love and misery. But Angélique was crying and sighing. Without looking up to see the sky I was trying to show her, she jumped in the water and floundered heavily as far as the beach, making the gulls and plovers flee with her large, angry gestures, as though to make them understand that they, even if they did not know it, were as responsible as Maurice, Charles, the bearded fat lady, the bull, the axe and the bottle for the world's ghastly unhappiness. I ran after her, more slowly than I wanted, thinking of a hundred pleasant things I would have liked to shout at her. On reaching the sand, I stood as though on an elder tree and shouted out, "But you're pretty, and tall, and educated! You hold your skirt like some Mary Magdalene, your eyes are as blue as the sky when it hasn't rained for six days! You are nice, and graceful, and if you didn't frighten the birds, they would perch on your shoulders to comfort you! Neither my father, mother sisters or brother or me wants to take an axe to your legs, or drink you until you're nothing more than an empty bottle, good just for hunters' target practice! You're complaining because words come to you easily! You could write letters, books, a *new* New Testament! You could light up our lives like some sort of sun! I don't know, you could, you could…"

Breathless, short of rare words, I stopped, convinced that Angélique had not heard my gibberish any more than had the lion in his cage or the apples on the apple tree, when I climbed it to tell the whole world what Mom called my "hothead's nonsense." But Angélique had come to a stop, and I saw her shoulders were shaking as though ants were running between her shoulder blades. She slowly turned around, staring at me with two eyes full of water, their blue tender as flax flowers. It was not me she was seeing, but a rag, a lost cat, the incarnation of one or another of her own dreams, and which made her feel pity. Suddenly she approached me, stretched forth her arm and caressed my head with the hand of a guardian angel wanting to remind you she is always there, and that no hole, no crevice will swallow up your poor body as it wanders around, forgetful of all danger. Above me, I heard her mumble as though saying a prayer to be heard by her alone, "You're really nice... You're really nice, Vallier!"

Then she let go of me and set off running with big strides along the beach. I lost sight of her when she crossed the point and plunged into the willows.

I often saw Angélique again. At mass, where she would twist her head to stare at me, looking like a school mistress determined to keep a close eye on the progress of a destiny more fragile than nice weather between two thunderclaps. On the ground outside the post office, which she exited with armfuls of mysterious packages that no one ever knew anything about, she would stop long enough to look down at me with a gaze that quickly grew tender then immediately hardened. She went off, shaking her head, as though the miracle she had glimpsed had just been a mirage, too beautiful to be true.

And then, one lovely June Sunday, the bells peeled far and wide, calling the parishioners to church. Angélique was getting married, for the first and last time. He: a certain Flavien Dagenais, a hired hand long as an elm and frizzly as a sheep, a sort of newcomer to our area who disconcerted everyone — except me, of course — with his John the Baptist hair and his Archangel Michael shoulders. People did not laugh much, nor tell dirty jokes, nor did they sing much at the wedding banquet, more mute than a funeral. The bride and groom sat motionless, solemn and embarrassed, at the very end of a big table to which people seemed to have been invited only to serve as witnesses to a marriage more miraculous than the wedding feast at Cana or the miracle of the loaves and fishes. We saw them disappear in an old, dilapidated, but washed, waxed, spick-and-span truck heading for a far-off village, both of them stiff and formal in their seats like prisoners being led away to be hung at the edge of a forest. There were no tin cans, no ribbons, no honking to salute the start of a honeymoon that left everyone pensive and discouraged, not even a cloud of dust in which we would have preferred to see them vanish, like the legendary team of beasts pulling "la Corriveau" and her accursed lover.

The rumour reached us, shortly thereafter, of a marital misfortune which everyone had foretold but whose violence exceeded the worst predictions. Flavien, it seemed, had taken to beating Angélique as hard as he could, with rakes and rifle butt. The crazed woman crossed through the village at night, uttering horrified laments full of words that returned like refrains, words from the past: bull, axe, bottle, wedding gown!

One day, as I was waiting for the train that would take me back home from college for the Easter holidays, I saw a tall, stooped woman climb aboard in front of me and gratify me in passing with a look that quickly turned forgiving and which I was not slow to recognize. I sat on the seat next to Anglique's and immediately tried to get her to remember me from distant memory. That woman watched me as if I was after the bag she was holding tight to her chest, as though it contained a bit of wood from Jesus' cross. Frightened, I cried out, "It's me, Vallier!"

She shrugged, suddenly waving an annoyed hand before her face as if to chase off a wasp that had been after her too long. I sat down, flabbergasted, and examined her out of the corner of my eye. She was Angélique, and was not Angélique. She was Angélique, present and yet vanished. All that remained of her was the posture of a school teacher tired of children, and a pair of eyes, blue like faded flax flowers. She got off the train at the next village where I was practically sure she had no business, carrying a final, mysterious package, containing, perhaps, the white gown which, for her agony, she had finally convinced her father to buy. Despite myself, I thought of the fat lady at the carnival, of my old lion in his cage, of Angélique's words, undeserved then as now: "You're really nice, Vallier!"

If I had been all that nice, I would have followed her, loved her, married her, I would not have let the bull, the axe, the bottle overcome that long, eccentric, fragile woman, vanished and irreplaceable. I remained in my seat, dreaming of chocolate, poaching, of no use for anything or to anyone, living only my life that brought pleasure and pain to me alone.

"You're really nice, Vallier!"

Yes, maybe. But, on the other hand, maybe not. That is probably what the lion was trying to tell me in his cage, even as I was trying to prove to him that he was still the handsome King of the Jungle, still fierce although already vanished, irreplaceable.

"You're really nice, Vallier!"

When you are truly nice, you open cages, destroy the axe, break the bottles, tether the bull back to its stake. If not, what's the point of being nice?

ROBERT LALONDE

My Nose Stuck Everywhere

With his head buried in the engine's night-dark depths, Dad was calling to me, "Vallier, can you tell me what that smell is?"

I came running; and, as Dad had, bent over the mysterious, rusty old metal that was shuddering and backfiring ominously, opened wide my nose holes, and immediately declared: "That's a piece of rope burning!"

Dad raised his head, banged it on the hood, swore between his teeth and finally, discouraged, retorted, "Come off it, Vallier, there's no rope in a tractor engine!"

I repeated, strangely sure of myself, "There's no mistake about it, no way: that's string being scorched!"

Dad looked at me as if he suspected some sort of frightful conniving with whatever devil was hiding in that clanging machine. I did not blink at his sceptical grimace, certain I was right. He dove back into the roaring cavern, rummaged around in the smoky guts of the engine for a while, and finally emerged with an indisputable, glowing piece of string. He contemplated it as though it were a miracle as

The Whole Wide World

implausible as Lazarus surging forth from his tomb. Triumphant, but modest ('cause Dad used to literally fume when I was a smart-aleck — "Vallier, don't act like you're Saint Dominic Know-It-All, it drives me nuts!") I murmured "Told you so!" more discreetly than a catechism response; and sprinted off, leaving him all alone, dumbfounded by the miracle. I could hear him muttering behind me, "Now you tell me: what the heck was that string doing in my engine?"

Edmond too used to seek my help to detect the presence of mould in his potions, or specify the degree of bitterness in one or another of his unfinished remedies. He would unscrew the lids of the row of jars on the workbench, and listen to me, all the while writing in a school notebook. I informed him of that trace of rotten rhubarb, curdled milk or cherry pit juice that had turned into turpentine and transformed his elixirs of life into dangerous poisons. Once I had proclaimed my diagnosis, in a voice suffocated by the toxic fumes rising from the jars, Edmond would open the shed door, furiously grab the pot of wasted magic and throw it against the stone wall at the edge of the field, where the flask often exploded like a grenade, giving off the sulphurous scent of skunk piss.

At the drop of a hat, Mom used to brandish the soup pot, the stew pot or a frypan of fricassee beneath my nose. Her eyebrows raised to the top of her forehead, she calmly awaited to learn if her sauce was short on salt, parsley, or whatever was left in the teapot. I often abused my power, going so far as to decree that a cup of brown sugar or a little glass of moonshine be added to the cake mix. Mom would then switch back to her usual face, that of a house wife whom the good Lord had not created "crazier than a broom-stick." and mutter pitilessly, "You can just do without this here supper, Vallier, if it's not to your taste!" and chased me away with the flick of a moist tea towel that pinched my thighs. I would leave the kitchen, red-cheeked: what if, on discovering that innocent little sin, Mom had conceived a horrific suspicion of all the evil I was capable of?

I sniffed and inhaled life around me with unwitting ardour, wrenching their precious essences from living things, gluttonously swallowing both the bloody odour of a pig being carved up, and the almond or cinnamon scent hidden beneath the skirts of the women in our home. My sister Anne, for example, behind each of her impatient hops on the porch, left a sour apple scent which made me imagine her squatting in the orchard, skirts pulled up onto her thighs, peeing on fallen apples. When Edmond was angry, he exuded burnt orange peel and rat poison, a bitter, complex odour like the stench floating over his concoctions. As for Alice, she smelled of faded chives and frozen pebbles. I used to spend hours on my hands and knees at the edge of the road, nose to the ground, my eyes closed tight like when I was taking Holy Communion, my hands clasped together behind my back, trying to distinguish between the scent of gravel and that of sand dust.

I would follow the dog's wanderings; stride hither and thither through forest, fields and swamp, the one Dad called "the quickswamp" because its black water bubbled as though thirty drowned corses lay permanently in the muck, together losing their breath which smelled like a heifer's fart.

The Whole Wide World

I did not separate out good and bad odours, every emanation was to me an aroma. Where others grimaced in disgust, pinched their nostrils when confronted with the carcass of a rotting woodchuck, an apple-for-the-road squashed at the side of that road, I used to open my nostrils wide, appreciating the subtle stench, assessing the surprising components of its fetidness, half crushed daisy heart, half cow fart: squatting over the carcass, I was in ecstasy. People would tug at my collar, tearing me away from my dirty sniffing, and push me along the road as one moves a mad calf away from the barbed-wire fence where the numbskull enjoys rubbing itself so much that it tears its hide till blood spurts out.

I sniffed at myself, rolled into a ball deep in my bed, at my arms, knees, armpits, magnetized by my skin's straw scent, the acrid odour of my body hair. I knew and recognized myself far more by my nose than by cogitation. I knew that I bore along with me, on a Lent morning, the scent of a freshly plucked duck; on a May evening, peach-perfumed breath; and on some winter nights, the subtle, generous perfume from between my buttocks, after a whole day spent on my school bench. When the snow was melting and the river thawing, I would flee the house and fall on all fours on the grass in the path, where only a woodchuck had crawled before me. With my snout at ground level, I meticulously inhaled the world's resurrection, following the scent of animals already awake. I could easily distinguish between the vanilla sweat of deer; and fox sweat, with its bitter, motor oil scent. I would bury my hands in hoofmarks, happy to feel the clay squirting between my fingers, freeing the young smell of bulrush shoots. On the beach, I flushed out extraordinary stinks: a rotted catfish lying in the mud, old reeds torn by the ice, faded crayfish shells between two mossy rocks, deer antler flavoured with black blood, wild cat carcass rotted by thaw, old water lily leaves clasping rocks, like scrawny hands.

A common cold — and I was no longer myself, floundering like a ghost in a funereal world smelling of starched cotton and straw dust. I used to dream that I continued to exist, in the void of odours lost and gone, like an embalmed corpse in its wadding. I saw others excitedly following their noses. The horse that caressed me smelled of dry paper, and a head of barley exhaled, as I passed by, the insignificant aroma of boiled cardboard. Animals seemed to struggle in a soporific, unhappy state, where I was unfortunately confined with them like a little Nativity scene character, a little plaster being, helpless and resigned.

As soon as the thick envelope, in which the flu had imprisoned me like a larva in its cocoon, began to fray, I darted into the fields, nostrils wide open, to salute, with moans and whistles, odours returned. The farmer who saw me from afar, jumping and shaking the branches in the path, must have thought I was a scarecrow escaped from its post and who no longer frightened but followed the birds just above the bulrushes; and was perhaps trying to fly off in their wake.

One April morning, my nose led me to river's edge, where I found him, run aground among the rotting branches in the bay.

I knew little of the Old Testament destiny of the village baker. Mr. Charbonneau, till then, had been a very ordinary creature who used to ride his bike by our place like a big, embarrassed little boy, his black tuque pulled down to his ears, winter and summer. To explain his unimportance on this earth, his cramped look, Mom used to say they were due to the torment he suffered from his wife and two daughters who were "plucking" the baker with their madly extravagant spending of every cent he earned baking his bread. The poor chap was rooted in front of his ovens all week long, "like a slave in chains." I as yet knew nothing then of destiny's dark joy when it tests its strength on the weakest among us. I had but an intuition, as fleeting and changing as a dragon glimpsed in a cloud, of the power of that dusk that began at the far edge of our horizon every day, and of the demons lying in wait for us at the bottom of the holes that our feet grazed daily. On that day, I was going to begin to understand those who explored the abyss on whose edge I occasionally roamed, as a butterfly hovers over a prickly burdock flower.

I pushed aside the reeds, and saw, firstly, a pair of shiny boots, Sunday footwear. I stretched out my arm to touch the polished leather of the boot that was steaming in the sunshine like a cake fresh from the oven. I was trembling, my fingers already knew that the feet in those boots would never wriggle again. I had often stared at sleeping feet, temporarily dead as they hung out of bed, or out of a cart stopped beneath a tree. But those boots were even more motionless, and I got scared. I backed up and fell seat first in the water, where my hand grazed the whitest, most tranquil hand I had ever seen, wide open, with pale nails, clean as those on church statues. People had hidden from me how peaceful were the gestures of the dead. That hand, lying tenderly open, almost graceful, was quite clearly that of someone set free. It no longer wanted to seize anything, strike anything, hold on to anything. The smooth palm allowed the water to flow, the cloud to fly freely by, the wind to blow on further. The hand was resting, infinitely. I was overcome by some slow giddiness, like that soft fall which, in dream, makes us descend like a damp cloth down a hole whose bottom we never touch. I knew the hand was dead; and that if I moved my arm further up, I would encounter the dead shoulder, the dead neck, the dead man's dead face. I did not move, but long remained by the deceased hand, motionless, horrified. A jay cawed in the branches, and that was like a signal: I at once opened my eyes and finally discovered the swollen face, the green ice of the eyes, the baker's bloated cheeks, so lean when he lived. A ribbon of algae was hanging out of blue lips half-opened on the black abyss of the mouth, where perhaps a bloodsucker was throbbing, or a tadpole was glued to the sticky ghost tongue. I allowed myself to utter the moan building up in me, and began to run in the water, between the slabs of mud-smeared ice. Only the sky and the branches could see me, and the clouds that calmly continued to move along, up there. I crumbled beneath a pine, for a long time breathing in the resin scent, the damp sand, the living grass. I re-visualized the strange dance I had just performed around the corpse, my mad deer's floundering about on the beach. I thought of Maurice Léger, the epileptic who, at the counter of the general store, would start to beat the air with both arms, and shake as though the Devil were after him, then fall stiff as a plank, foam on his chin, howling frightful pleas in a language he alone understood. When the Angel and Jacob wrestled, the Angel always won. But Maurice would finally awake, pale as a ghost. Ignoring the play-acting he had just gesticulated before our eyes, he took coins out of his pocket to pay for his tobacco, and picked up his hat, fallen between chair legs. Whereas Mr. Charbonneau remained lying in the mud, watching the clouds go by without seeing them, breathing air that no longer smelled of anything, letting water flow over his hand without its coolness disturbing him.

And the sun came out from behind a cloud, its vast golden light streaming forth over the water and among the trees. The river shivered, became spiked with whitecaps, the wind jumped among the branches which sighed deeply. The whole bay proclaimed the impossibility of death. The gulls soared over the drowned man, always uttering the same cries which mocked the corpse in the mud. I, alone, knew.

Never would Mr. Charbonneau go back home. His ovens would no longer release, throughout the whole village on Saturday mornings, the sacred aroma of rising bread. The birds flew hither and thither, the wind was blowing, the sun kept shining. And I was inhaling deeply, sniffing at the pine gum, the sap of the bulrushes, the honey-bee clover, my own sweat with its subtle stench of marsh trillium. A voice in me murmured to the Good Lord, "We are here, in this bay, alone in the world, because you put us here, and one day, you will take us back. That's all, there's nothing else…" It was terrible, but very simple. There was nothing more to see, nothing left to imagine. All was included in that thought: suffering, desire, innocence, all our fears, spiders' madness in the grass, wild cats' voraciousness, the slowness of egg-laden carps in the stream, the houses we build, the fervour of prayers, the words one says, those one writes to ward off grief; illness, the wide eyes we open beside the dead who make us fall to our knees before infinity. Ecstasy; and then collapse: such was fate, and not otherwise.

I leaped up, like someone resuscitated. Without so much as a glance at the corpse, I ran for the village. I progressed without feeling the sand nor the pebbles beneath my feet, pushed on by that haste, that pride angels feel as they fly to relate their dramatic tales.

The villagers immediately recognized in me the messenger wearing a halo identifying him from afar. Everyone would run to the porch of the general store to listen to me recite, my voice changed by the truth, waterside death. Smothered by horror, however, my voice did not obey me. I could only manage to mutter confused babblings that made them think I had fallen on my head, or that a furious dog had chased me a long way, biting my heels.

"Catch your breath, little guy, then start at the start."

They sat me on a bench and brought me a large glass of water that I swallowed down in one gulp as though I had just got out of a barn on fire. Then they formed a circle around me, like the Temple Priests around young Jesus. Seeing their long faces, their drooping pipes, their squinting eyelids, I was stricken by sudden idiocy and lost all my inspiration. I simply mumbled, "Mr. Charbonneau is lying in the mud, at the head of the bay."

The men lowered their heads in unison to examine their boot tips, then spread out, bellowing curses and commands. I saw them harness themselves to a rope stretcher, and plunge into the branches. I could not find anywhere within me the courage to follow them. I was like a flame that suddenly goes out in the frightening darkness of a church. My exaltation had departed, like a dream when you put a foot out of your bed. Were they going to punish me for not having run fast enough? On seeing the signs of my shuffling on the beach, would the men discover the craziness that had made me waste time?

Suddenly, the women came out of their homes, one by one, and surrounded me on the porch, asking me a thousand questions, urging me to relate in detail my discovery of the drowned man in the moss. I stammered, got mixed up, talked about his brand-new boots, his open hand in the water, the strand of algae between his teeth; but no longer feeling the madness that had taken hold of me just a little earlier, on the beach. Then the women turned away from me, sat down on the stairs, and began to talk.

"Often you're heading straight for trouble when you chatter with the Devil, all alone in your corner…"

"Pride may be a bad sin, okay; but you have to have a bit of it, so you can stand up to frenzied profiteers…"

"Especially profiteers in skirts, you mean! It's just so appalling!"

"Gnawing, gobbling, can't tell gold from pebbles, all they care about is parading around…"

"Still, if the guy would've had the backbone to stand up to them!"

"Oh, in that department, he was pretty spineless…"

"A real lazybones, ready more often than not to let himself be fleeced, and then plot his revenge while he crisscrossed the village on his damn bicycle!"

"That's not so sure!"

"Whadya mean, not so sure?"

"That little guy was way too dumb to plot anything!"

"Come off it! I know that kind of guy. Take Aurèle…"

"Oh, don't you start up about your Aurèle! To listen to you, he sounds like some kind of angel fallen from Heaven above just to split your wood and take a scythe to your big pasture…"

"I'll have you know…"

"Not a thing! Something was eating away at our baker, and we'll never know what! And that's all there is to it."

I was Ulysses attached to his mast, forced to listen to those mermaids whom I could neither join nor drive off by hitting them hard with a plank. Worse, as I was listening to them, my nose picked up the smells of cookie dough, gooseberry jam and syrupy donuts emanating from these be-skirted tale-tellers. I was desperate, and hungry. I was ashamed, and shivering with appetite, with the desire to return to my room, my books, the unbelievable magic of invented stories. But the funereal chatter went on and on, and the men had not returned with the drowned corpse. I closed my eyes, and saw them pushing big blocks of rust-coloured ice with their boots, someone grabbing a foot, another an arm, someone else the nape of the neck, and them all pushing him onto the beach. One knelt on the moist sand, another signed himself, and a third grimaced as he scratched his shoulder.

So it was possible to scorn too good a person, to such an extent that he came to hate his own kind nature; and no longer appeared in the village except as a ghost persecuted by starlings? Was it that misery that made his face look like some scoffed-at child's, and gave his eyes that disillusioned look which sometimes stopped upon me, as though I were an angel's shadow beside the road? So it was possible to be the only one to know that others' hearts were capable of anything, and the only one, yet again, to suffer the results? So the guy had chosen his own martyrdom? Neither drink, nor anger, nor prayer, nor God nor the Devil had been beseeched? The baker had believed in nothing, and endured his torment as though guilty, atoning for some great, unknown sin? Which one? I racked my brains in vain, recalling the tales of the baker's comings and goings: I found nothing which could justify the shame he bore everywhere, like mourning garb. Had the poor man made a pact with the Devil, hoping to see one of the women drop dead; or, even worse, hoping to discover a knife in his hand and enough courage in his arm to plunge it into those skirts and put an end to his shame, in an appalling chaos of blood, flour, and the hellish heat of his oven? Supposing he clambered onto his old bicycle to exhort the dry trees and the crows, Satan's lackeys, to hasten his deliverance?

Mr. Charbonneau, after baking his bread, had got on his bike. As usual, he had taken the sandy path, had skirted round the ice-edged puddles as far as the trail running through the willows where, just the day before, he had stopped. But that morning, the bicycle entered the water, and Mr. Charbonneau remained on the seat, back straight, his eyes staring at the already frozen river. He was wearing his everyday suit, but his Sunday boots; and his pockets were stuffed with stones. Why had he wanted to depart wearing his brand-new boots?

"I knowed it!"

"You knowed what?"

"That it had to happen! Last Sunday, the sanctuary lamp suddenly went out, while the priest was reading the Scriptures…"

That was Mom. I wished I could dig a hole in the sand at the foot of the stairs and bury myself in it forever.

They found the bicycle the next spring. An old, dilapidated, rusty machine inside a big block of ice, on the beach in front of the school.

THE WHOLE WIDE WORLD

Your Mother Has a Visitor

Mom enjoyed sitting among the shadows, talking about things good, and things bad; about what is worth something, sometimes worth gold; or what is worth nothing, not even shit; and about what makes you happy, or sad. Her hands on the worn arms of her armchair, at dusk, in the dim living room, she would whisper, when she saw me stand up to turn on the switch, "No, Vallier, don't turn on the light! It's soothing to guess what things are, instead of them jumping out at you…"

I would sit back down beside her, whom I could scarcely make out in the half-light of autumn at five P.M., Mom's favourite season and time of day. Then, worries, work, and the sad thought that peace still and always failed to reign on Earth, all faded away, replaced by the carefree, gently blurred evening as it fell. I had no idea what to say in that darkness which turned our house into a cave, transforming our mother into some murmuring stranger speaking as much to night itself as to me, hunkered in my corner. Wary of the trouble that arose on such evenings, I tried to prevent it by chatting away about ordinary things, not at all supernatural. But Mom had other intentions. She would spend that murky hour in weird confessions that, like a string of bad news, made my stomach gurgle and churn. We do not always know why certain words surprise us, why we suddenly become sad on hearing them, even words we know by heart and which sometimes flush out doves, and sometimes crows. Mom, with a hushed voice, would relate to me the chronicle of all things possible and impossible, things true, things false, some man's dangerous ardour, some woman's undeserved disappointment; going from the sunshine of a birth — in a house I'd never set foot in and which she described to me meticulously, as though she had spent her whole youth there — to a death which grieved her as though she had been the deceased's first cousin. At such times, I visited unimaginable living-rooms where the carpets and couches were arranged so outlandishly, kitchens where the stove and sink were so crazily close, that I came to wonder if the poor people who lived in those incomprehensible thatched huts wore skirts and pants like us, and obeyed the same implacable superstitions. Perhaps we were a distinct species? Maybe we were the eccentric, peculiar, mysterious ones, with our strange joys, our unique misfortunes, our preposterous beliefs?

But Mom did not let me wonder long about the mysterious disparities which made each family in the village an unknowable clan, with its own privileges and misdeeds, its *thou shalts* and *thou shalt nots*. She had so much to tell me, to teach me. "Léa Guindon won't be living high off the hog any more. And it's not because, as your father would put it, she's bought felt boots! The poor woman has a bad heart. She fell down twice on her way back from high mass. Eudore Thivierge picked her up, in front of the Lauzon's barn…"

And, in the obscurity, she would sigh her collector-of-incidents-and-accidents sigh. One word after the other, she unburdened herself of her overload of useless knowledge of others' lives, which she was powerless to change other than by describing them as she pleased, in detail and at length. "Eudore lost his wife just before Halloween, so Louisa Dumoulin — who always celebrates Easter before Palm Sunday, of course — led him and Laura Lafleur before the altar to exchange wedding bands for better and especially for worse… Eudore, who drinks like a fish, doesn't do his laundry, never does the housework… The first two steps of his porch fell in at least six months ago: now is that any way to live? The milkman twisted his ankle when he was delivering Eudore's milk, last week… And you know it never rains but it pours…"

Suddenly flustered, losing track of the up and downs of everyone's lives, Mom seemed to sink into a deep trap, unnoticed the minute before, and that was closing down on top of her — on her alone, she whose own existence was never included in the tangled tales of good and bad luck she told. At such moments, I could hear a tragic, unusual tone in her voice which sunk to a murmur — as though she was swallowing her words back down so as to be the only one to hear them whispering next to her heart. Abruptly panicking at the inexplicable silence falling between us, I would utter, in a murmur also, words I hoped were inoffensive and might encourage her to continue, to let it all out — I could tell she was chock-full; and that her inner burden had imprisoned her heart like a field mouse in a bag of grain.

"What are you looking at, Mom?"

"For Heaven's sake, now you tell me, how in the world can Jean-Louis Vézina have so much to tell Germaine Côté? He's always over there. Since she hasn't got curtains any more — Germaine is so proud of the floral satin on her new couch that she'd like everyone to stare at it like it was a mirror — any Christian passing by can see them both, side by side on that couch, grabbing each other's hands and gabbing on and on... Ah, love, damn love! It makes you talk, and especially cry, you know..."

The naked maple tree in the window would gesticulate desperately, and leaves swirled about the field like scales fallen from the eyes of the Good Lord himself. As soon as I saw people overtaken by the distress of being at the end of their tether, I started to feel the fatigue of our exile, the insignificance of our dreams and desires. Neither the first snowfall, which at any moment would be falling on our fields, nor the Nativity scene we would soon set up beneath our glittering Christmas tree, nor the music, nor the tourtières, nor the presents, nor even the fierce urge to go down the hill on a sled could convince me that our days were not numbered, that something would follow our earthly life; nor that the heavy, almost motionless heart in my chest was not a rock which, like a day-dreaming scatter-brain, I had hitherto thought was a brave muscle functioning on its own.

"When you try so hard to help others, sometimes it's

worse than if you'd done nothing... That reminds me, have you noticed your sister Anne's new cape? She cut that rag from a tablecloth that I'd stored in the attic to keep it clean. Your father thinks it makes her look like a Madonna. I say it makes her look more like Maria Goretti than the real Maria Goretti. Gotta say that, aside from driving us daft with her crazy music, your sister isn't gifted for much. Mind you, she isn't the first nor the last such "prodigy" to show up in this neck of the woods! But she has a kind heart, you've got to grant her that. Just yesterday, a whole month before the holiday season, she polished all my silverware — the set that came from my mother, your Grand-mother Lachance. You remember her, of course?"

"A little. One Christmas, she gave me two dollar bill rolled up inside a tie..."

"Which you've never worn, as we know full well! The gentleman is as stylish as a beadle! But as for the two bucks, the Devil knows where they went! By the way, you are actually listening to me? Now, that's new!"

"No way. I listen to you all the time, Mom."

"Go tell that to the toads, they'll swallow you down like a fly, my little guy."

Then, suddenly, "Winter's coming! I don't feel up to it, Vallier! I don't feel up to anything any more..."

"Up to what, Mom? Halloween's over, soon we'll have a merry little snowfall; and then it'll be Christmas..."

"You can't understand, Vallier..."

Understand what? That, for her, time was passing both too fast and too slowly, that it was leaving everything unfinished, unfinishable, that our existence was constantly making promises and breaking them? That we were all, she like the rest of us, angels with clipped wings, demons with splintered pitchforks, adventurers in a very long purgatory from which, not even in dream, the boldest of the sleepers we were could ever escape? What was there behind, below, beyond an unforgiving Fate that left us short of breath, took away all our carefree feelings, all our pleasure at existing among trees and things?

One evening in early November — I had just turned fifteen and thought I had finally finished being held prisoner like a young calf tethered in its stable — Mother went completely nuts. For starters, we heard the noise of some extraordinary housework above us. Seated in the living room, hands on our knees, we heard chairs dancing, closet doors slamming, bed feet trotting across the floor and making heavy, sand-thick dust rain down on us. Dad — who seemed to know what demented demon had started to possess Mom — declared, twisting his mouth around his pipe stem, "Your mother has a visitor, I do believe."

"Weird visitor!"

Edmond, pale as the underside of a vine leaf, was blinking his eyes, his teeth chattering. Any disturbance in the mathematical progression of time and acquired habits made him itch, like a mistake in his calculations. Anne, her eyebrows raised, was chewing her nails and singing a bizarre melody I was sure she would never be able to recall. Alice was continuously rubbing the arms of her armchair, as if to thwart the snow falling from the ceiling from settling in for a long, very sad winter. Upstairs, things were getting shoved around, housework was getting done. Now and then, we could hear an unrecognizable voice, raging, then laughing, then angry again, proclaiming a whole string of riddles with neither rhyme nor reason, peppered with moans in which distress and sensual pleasure were indistinguishable.

The only explanation Dad gave, without our even asking, was whispered: "Your mother's going through her change of life, children, her *retour d'âge!*"

The change of life, a calamity for Mom, a mystery to me, was attacking our household. But: where had it gone, this age that was "returning" to us? Was it Mother's childhood, her youth, starting over again — reclaiming her body, babbling with her voice, screaming the pain of along-ago teething — mysteriously reborn, laughing the un-motivated laugh of a newborn rocking itself all alone in its crib?

Mom was beginning a long martyrdom, a depression that no one in our family would henceforth designate otherwise than by that imprecise, allegorical and time-honoured expression: the visitor. Mom was visited often indeed, at all hours of the day and night, awake or asleep, whether lying sweat-soaked in the middle of her bed, or sitting on a birch-shaded stump in the middle of the pathway leading to the sugar shack where, before the visitor arrived, she never set foot, fearing snakes and flies. Apparently, her tyrannical demons also protected her from all the ordinary hassles which, during her life as an everyday run-of-the-mill woman, used to put her in a terrible state.

And then one evening, at the supper table, when I was alone with her — Dad had returned to the stable, Anne and Edmond to school and Alice to the neighbours' who had hired her as a maid — Mom, while absent-mindedly moving her fork about in a little swampy island in her beef and carrot stew she had scarcely touched, stared at me as though I was one or another of the mysterious incarnations that, at any moment, suddenly loomed up in her face.

"Vallier, don't forget the flowers!"

"But what flowers, Mom?"

"On my grave. Lots of flowers, especially rudbeckias, you know how much I loved them…"

My heart dropped to the pit of my stomach: the rudbeckias would outlive Mom, tall and straight, flourishing on her grave, and what's more: thanks to me. That gardening, which I did not understand, demoralized me. I did not know, did not yet understand that Mom was initiating me — unknowingly and, even more, unintentionally — to the exalted, generous, very dangerous complicity that swells ordinary disappointments into soul-eating tragedies. I was taking onto myself the injustice and horror of her sudden despair. I imagined myself swinging hard axe blows at the clock glass, breaking it, unsure whether I should move the needles of time forward or back. Yesterday, tomorrow, a minute ago or hence were happy, carefree moments. I wished that, with a magician's sweeping, infallible flourish, I could make the snow fall, and then melt, hurrying spring along. I would have liked to jump ahead of our sluggish pace prey to fatal, insane torpors. I wished I could leave the house carrying Mom on my back, light as a bunch of old clothes, carefully sit her down beside me on the truck seat and quickly set off, smiling from ear to ear, for those countries where they danced with flowers in their hair, and carefree minds. I wanted to scamper off with her to those far corners of the world she used to describe, sighing like someone walled up alive, some evenings, looking through magazines borrowed from Yvette Dupré, the hairdresser. Those faraway worlds were, of course, accessible. Pages in the magazines promised to take us to those paradises of blue seas and bewitched dancing, for money which I would earn even if I had to work till my arms fell off. She would wear a silk dress and be supple as a vine, while I danced with her on the marble of ancient temples; for her I would steal pineapples from market stalls, rush down ravines crawling with snakes and bring back to our little hut beneath the palm trees that bottle of fire-water, that elixir able to make us forget everything. I was ready to do anything, but capable of nothing. I was enduring a frightening desire to soar up and beyond, as I sat before her like some chastised angel, a trickster so absent-minded he had let his power escape. Because my mind had been on something else the day, the hour, the second when I should have cast the spell, recited the magic sentence, formulated my wish, Mom was shipwrecked like an old boat, its bottom smashed, in the mud of a shallow spot where I would be in danger of drowning were I to dive in and try rescuing her. That shipwreck was worse that the sinking of the Titanic. I glimpsed dark sea abysses in the depths of the living room, and thought I could make out monsters, their gaping mouths bristling with pointed teeth, among the grimaces the setting sun cast on the walls. Everything around us was dying, everything was ending, everything was vanishing. We were sinking, being carried off in a lethal, sluggish whirlpool dragging us down into a sort of hell under the house, under life, under calm normality. I was discovering, mute and almost feverish, the opposite of everyday existence, a world where everything is already finished without having ever started: that limbo where unuttered secrets, the ashes of desire and tenderness, the muffled footfall of our miserable wanderings in a real less certain than our dreams, awaited us. It was autumn, an autumn that would not become winter, a long, mad, empty time where we would soon cease to know one another, ghosts among spectres, shapeless, odourless matter drifting along in our ragged clothes. We were dead, worse than dead, paralysed zombies, our eyes gaping at the great, empty truth of absence.

"Vallier, are you thinking what I am, do you see what I see?"

Of course I was thinking of the same nothingness, and seeing the same colourless life: I was with her in the same pale otherworld where I no longer could recognize anything and that seemed to go on forever. With a horrific effort, I freed my tongue from the thick dish towel wrapped around it, and just barely managed to mumble, "We musn't give up, Mom..."

I said "we" because we were now in the same boat which neither of us could save from sinking. Already stuck, caught in an eddy, I was going down with Mom, a part of her shipwreck. Black muck was filling the living room, the unlit lamps watched our tranquil descent into hell where everything weighs on you, but not a thing matters any more. A subterranean refuge offering no shelter at all, into which I am still often forced to fall, even today, spellbound by Mom's muffled voice muttering in the dark, "Nothing, there's nothing left, not a thing matters to me any more, nothing serves any purpose..."

The lament of someone fallen out with life, abandoned by angels and demons alike, the sigh of a drifter watching herself float slowly away. A daze described by poets, scorned by normal folk and put up with by those close to you, who can do nothing more for you, who glimpse you from far, far away, like a drowned body way out in the open sea: such is that dazed state, whose every minute lasts a century.

One morning, Mom hung out her laundry on the clothesline, humming a tune by the "Singing Madman," Charles Trenet, and smiling at the clouds. The visitor had left, the living room was devoid of ghosts, the spectres had vanished. The dog was barking and jumping at her, and Mom was scolding it, her voice full of laughter and forgetfulness. The spell was over, her nerves had untangled themselves like a ball of fishing line you've patiently conquered. Spring was falling from the branches, shadows stretched out innocently on the grass.

I sat down on the bottom step of the stairs and looked at her, flabbergasted, not yet sure that the halo of light around her would not change into a cloud darting lightning bolts. But Mom, cured, young, happy, free at last, was smiling, eyes and mouth.

"Why are you looking at me like that, Vallier? You're as pale as what the cat's dug up three times this morning!"

And she was laughing so hard that the birds fled from the mountain ash. Then I climbed up to the attic and returned to their chests and closets the showy paraphernalia of her consultations with the visitor: the yellowed wedding gown; pictures from her youth — which showed Mom sitting on some unknown swing in some unknown garden; old, faded straw purses; bottles of perfume gone flat; long, faded ribbons; and a lock of very blond hair wrapped in tissue paper. The trappings of unhappiness were no longer in season, and I too was smiling as I did my housework. That summer's light would never end.

Still, I remained cautious: I returned to sit on the step, feeling a slight fear that might have rekindled her suspicions. But Mom was still smiling and chattering happily away: "Your Aunt Alice will be here for the picnic! They're going to let her leave the convent! I'll have to lend her a dress, that yellow one that fastens at the neck. The poor girl has hair all the way down to below her calves, it's a fright to see!…"

She was laughing, shaking shirts and pants, from which, like snow, fell the dry scales of monsters slain.

The Whole Wide World

The End of the World

I used to scrape holes in the snow to see pine roots running along the ground, rust-coloured needles, a few black fern leaves in the depths of their so silent grottos beneath the thick white layer. Everywhere, always, there were hiding places, dens, nests and secret spots, attics perched up high, basements nested under the ground we walked on top of all day long like birds with clipped wings. I used to scratch, excavate, bury myself beneath the moss, chafe my knees on oak trunks: I always had to see the world from high above or deep below, convinced I had been born to know intimately both the silvery dust of the northern lights and the black, dead waters of subterranean rivers. I felt my life would be but a short day in the world, a quick excursion: there was too much to see, smell, touch, discover. I was not afraid I would fall, be swept away by an eddy, or smash my body on a craggy rock: I was afraid of lacking time. I feared, for example, that I would never reach the end of the field where a stone giant rose high, "The Miracle Maker" turned into a statue after thinking he was Almighty God; or else the hill crest where eagles supped, perched upright on the dead branches of the "mastodont," that oversized ash as impressive, to us, as a cathedral. The universe was too big and my movements too slow. I was lagging, crawling, when I should have been running, flying, walking on water, striding over the village houses and leaping into the galaxies.

I knew my steps in the county were counted the day I emerged into the clearing where horses pastured, and found myself face to face with old Périard who was announcing the end of the world to the hares and spruce, his arms raised high, his tall, skinny body shaking in gusts of wind, though none were stirring the foliage.

"Evil sinners with your mortal sins, little sinners with your venial sins, carefree fools in this county and in the whole wide world, you're dreadfully naive! This world's soon going to split in two and swallow you down like caterpillars!... It's going to rain upside-down, thunder down below, snow sideways, and get so freezing it'll split your skulls before you can raise your hand to your forehead to start crossing yourselves!... Oh you complacent, miserable sinners, your insignificant lives are about to end! Poor, poor, happy-go-lucky sinners damned to fire and brimstone!..."

So many catastrophes came from his twisted mouth that a long stream of spittle ran down his neck, saliva as green as a calf's cud in a pasture. I squatted in the shade of a willow tree, already shivering myself, my breathing shallow, the nape of my neck prickling with fright. For I had often thought about the end of this dangerously stretched-thin recess we call life. For quite a while now, I had been waiting for the whistle to blow, the valve to bang shut, the creaking gate to close. Sooner or later, I was well aware, the door of our paradise would slam shut in my face. Rolled up in a ball at the foot of the willow, I felt my veins fill with a fatal poison that had circled my heart a thousand times without stopping and was killing me today with a sudden, murderous squirt. You run in the field, a calm person under a death sentence, a dying amnesiac, a mad pony that does not know it is galloping with death as its bridle. And then, suddenly, your feet are going over the cliff, you're already tumbling, you pedal in a void and the birds pay us no more attention than if we were rocks rolling full speed down a mountain. We have not lived, have barely become able to stand like the colt born that very morning, and already we are crumbling like so many lead-riddled grouse, cut stems, puppies drowned by the storm in their hole under the shed.

I did not know much about old Périard, except that Dad had told me he was "a river-man." I used to imagine him, of course, just come out of the water, a fish-man, a big talking crab stranded one morning on the beach between smooth wood shavings and rotting algae: some sort of monster with its scales torn off, out of its element among our trees, our air and especially us, strange humans conceived and born on land. Most certainly, his speech was underwater, bubbling like an eddy in quicksand, sucking you down and drowning you. The river-man — whom I imagined had been taught by some god of the currents, some sand-bar oracle — was prophesying the end of our world that had surged out of the water too long ago, our great earthly park wherein dense schools of gill-less sinners were swimming upright, not counting their breaths, gripped by an illusion of eternity which, for sure, would be their undoing. I could see all that, old Périard surging forth like a Leviathan from the big lake, his face streaked with mud and bulrush juice, emerging at the head of the bay to warn us of the terrible tidal wave that would sweep us back into our original silt. My imagination was biblical, and, of course, horrified, at age eleven. The fable of Adam and Eve struggling with the cursed worm hidden in the apple had instilled in me a subtle shame that flowed endlessly with my blood. Perhaps I would be the first to be swallowed down, since I ceaselessly took great bites out of the apple, my mouth full of the sweetish saliva of a glutton madly satiating himself. Mother would often tell me, "You want too much, Vallier! The apple, the basket, the whole apple tree, and while you're at it the whole orchard, and even the neighbour's orchard! For heaven's sake, be a little less greedy! You'll die from pulsating desire, from huge, unattainable ambition!..."

Pulsating desire, huge unattainable ambition, the infinite terror to wind up not having had enough apples, wind, summer, that gentle blue, grey or green human gaze, true love, abundant and yet so hard to find.

Suddenly I was discovering that my supplies would soon be cut off, and also, at the same time, air, desire and fear. Far from seeing the end of my martyrdom, I could glimpse the long boredom of nothingness, unending deprivation, the limbo of the Great Void after my life, when I would continue to exist — I could not imagine disappearing, going off; but, worse, remaining alone in world turned upside down and where I would know everything had disappeared forever — the white of my eyes widened, my ribs visible just beneath my skin and my brain forever bonkers.

My voice sounded like the scatterbrained chirping of a bird: "When exactly is it going to happen?"

The only answer was the wind in the branches. The old man had perhaps disappeared: I had mediated a long time, beneath the willow. I sat up, pushed aside the leaves and saw an ordinary, elderly man, his eyes empty, his mouth open, his hemp-hued locks scolded by the breeze. The prophet looked uncannily similar to any oldster out for his constitutional in the woods. "What are *you* doing here?"

His whole body was discouraged now, shoulders and arms drooping, dead — two dry branches pointed down at the moss — arms which a few minutes ago were churning in the sky like the wings of Lucifer. I did not get flustered: he had said too much, or not enough, and I wanted to know the very day, the exact time when the world would disappear: "Just when is the end of the world coming?"

This time he laughed, or, rather, whinnied, his mouth gaping: a long roar that made two grouse fly off behind him. Then his madness suddenly stopped, as though he had only wanted to scare the birds, as he had frightened me. A scarecrow, maybe that's what he was, after all, that old man, a stuffed prophet to keep the starlings at a distance and frighten children. It was only when he had sunk back into the brush that he answered me, the grouse and the wild grasses in the clearing: "It's already started, and you know it!"

I stood stock still, trembling aspen among the aspen trembling in the wind, right in the middle of the end of the world already under way, the squabbling clearing surrounded by the crickets' *Dies irae*.

The next Sunday, at nine o'clock mass, between the pages of my missal, a page torn from his with these three words scribbled in pencil: *Are you ready?*

In the sand of the little bay, one afternoon, drawn with a stick, a gigantic exterminating angel, sword brandished — an alder branch — over its dishevelled head.

One red August evening, in the little tin jar in the bottom of the boat, his grimy scapular wrapped in a newspaper page bearing the handwritten words, *It will come any day now!*

Then, of course, I returned to the clearing. He was awaiting me, beneath the willow. It was Sunday, September 4, 1958. How could I forget that day when I had gone to meet the end of the world so often announced? The falling raindrops were so tiny you could not see them, and the crickets had fallen silent in the grass. Pale as a sheet, he was waiting for me.

"I suppose you've finally understood!"

He was stretched out on the moss. His missal was in his pocket; I had his scapular in mine. But we did not have time to recite the prayers. The whole thing did not last long, the old angel was so tired: a dislocated scarecrow that no longer frightened either me or the birds.

Why me? Because I was the one who scraped holes in the snow, climbed every tree, read letters not meant for me, and wanted to jump into the galaxies? Because I was the one who sensed so clearly the approaching end that it did not frighten me?

His modest tombstone bore these simple, graven words:

Auguste Périard, 1879-1958, Requiescat in pace.

I closed his eyes, and then long listened to the rain. I was still alive, mysteriously. I was alive, but running short of time, of course, time which the old prophet had lost. Time that is a god, the only one we have left. It will not let itself be swayed, lengthened, nor shrunk. Eternal for some, long dead for others, perhaps Time is that open-armed angel, awaiting us, on the other side.